Between the Pipes

STORY BY **Albert McLeod**
WITH **Elaine Mordoch** AND **Sonya Ballantyne**
ART BY **Alice RL**

HIGHWATER
PRESS

To all the 2SLGBTQI+ people who were forced to let go, and those who continue to hold on to forge a path forward. —ALBERT MCLEOD

To the research participants who shared their stories to better life for the next generation. —ELAINE MORDOCH

To Manon Rhéaume, who got me into hockey. —SONYA BALLANTYNE

I dedicate this book to my parents and my friends. —ALICE RL

To the wallflowers of locker rooms and libraries. —KIELAMEL SIBAL

———————————————

Content Warning: This book includes scenes that engage with homophobia and toxic masculinity, which could be difficult for readers, especially those within the 2SLGBTQI+ community. If you are in crisis in Canada or the United States, please call or text the Suicide Crisis Helpline at 988, or visit itgetsbettercanada.org for more support resources in your region. Further resources can be found at the back of this book.

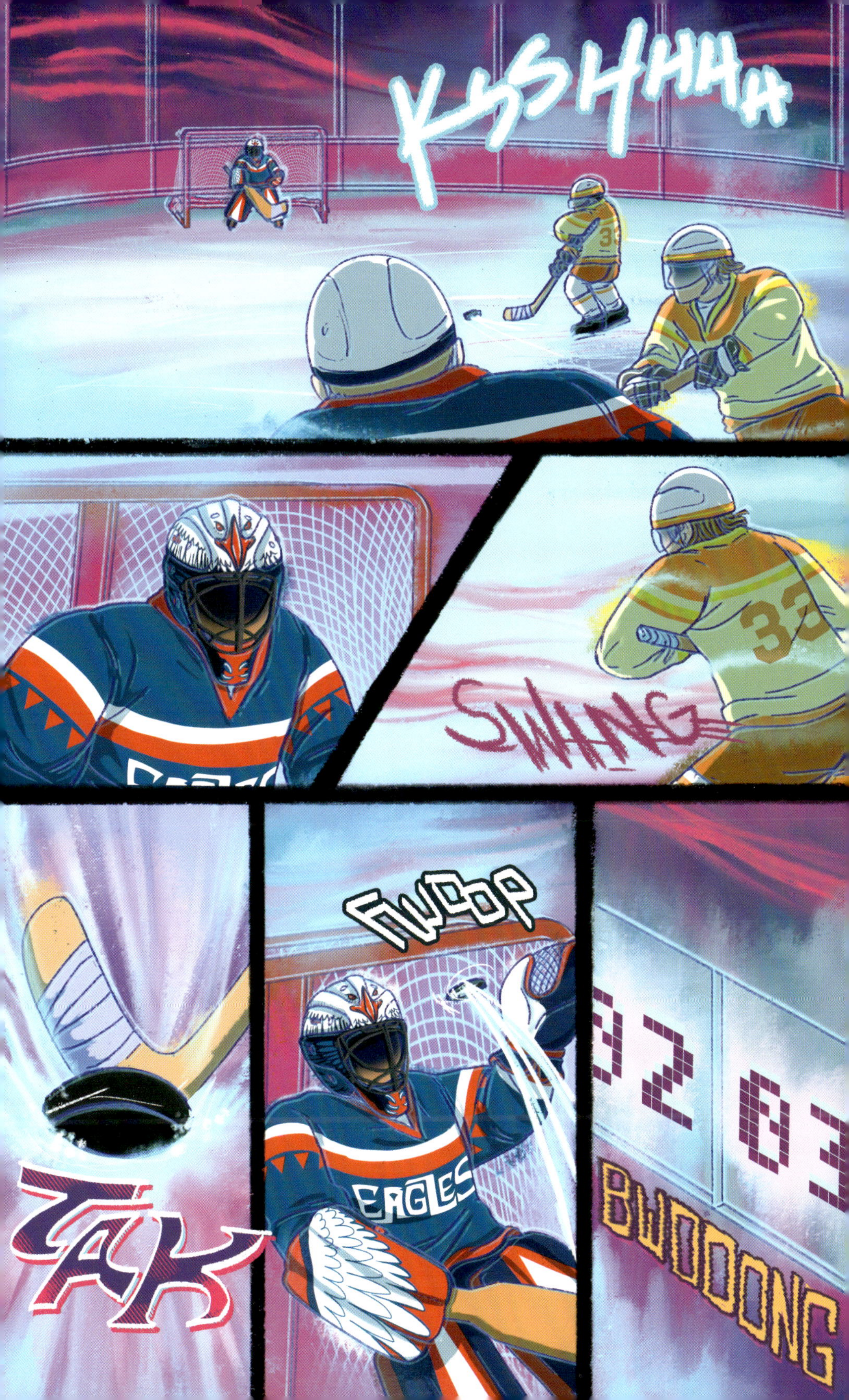
KSSHHHH
SWANG
TAK
FWOOP
BWOOOONG

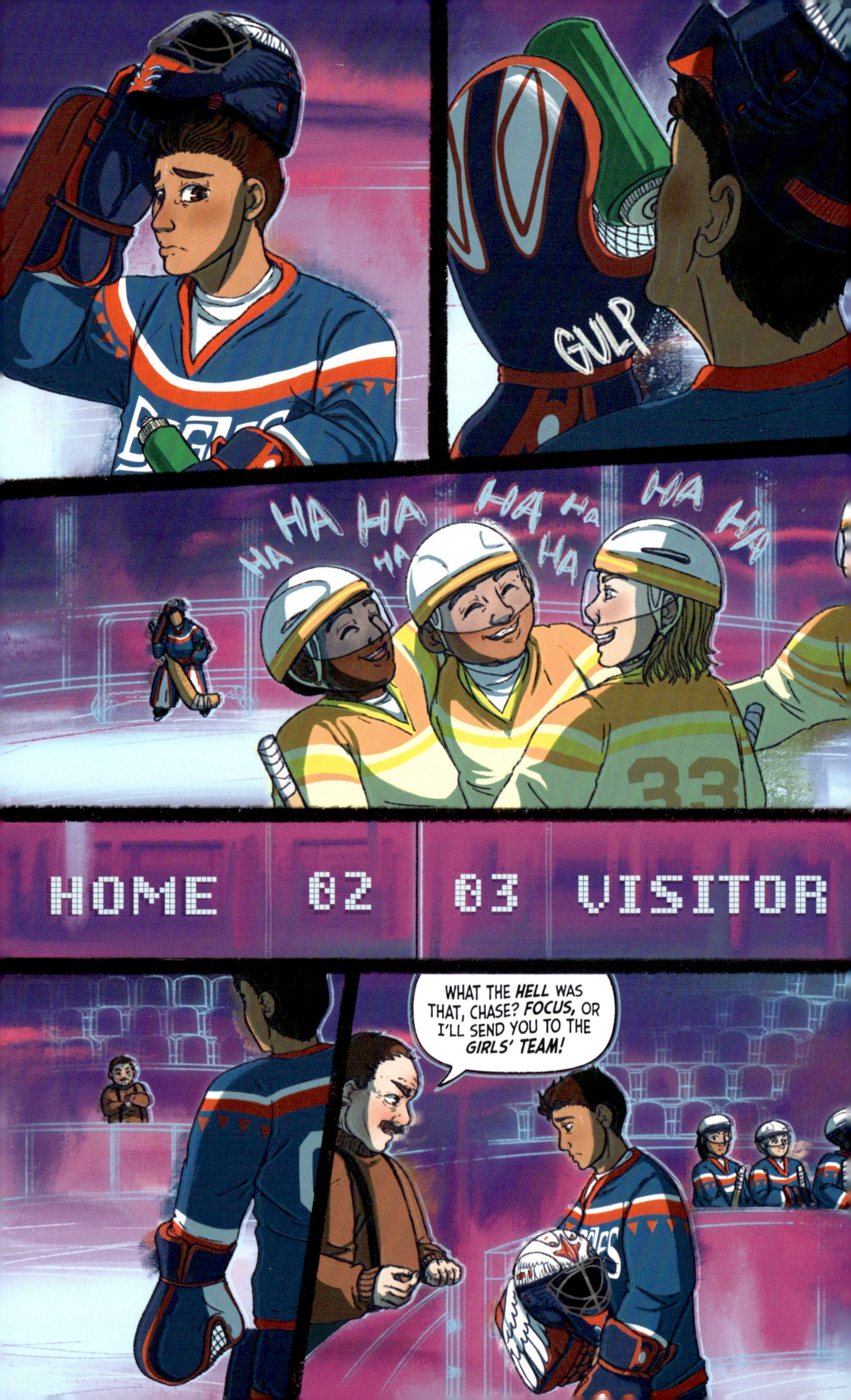

GULP
HA HA HA HA HA HA HA HA HA HA HA
HOME 02 03 VISITOR
WHAT THE HELL WAS THAT, CHASE? FOCUS, OR I'LL SEND YOU TO THE GIRLS' TEAM!

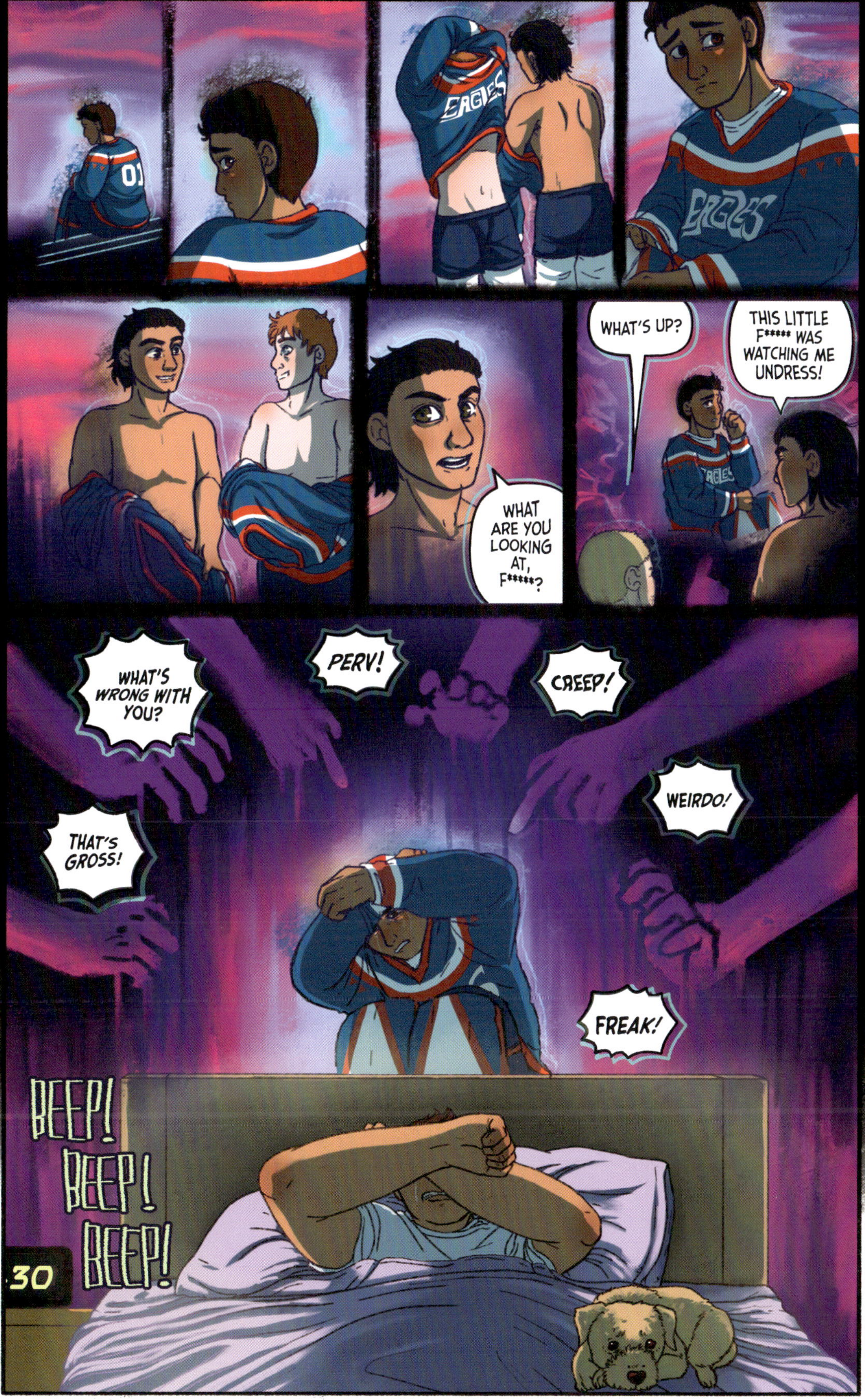
WHAT ARE YOU LOOKING AT, F*****?
WHAT'S UP?
THIS LITTLE F***** WAS WATCHING ME UNDRESS!
WHAT'S WRONG WITH YOU?
PERV!
CREEP!
WEIRDO!
THAT'S GROSS!
FREAK!
BEEP! BEEP! BEEP!

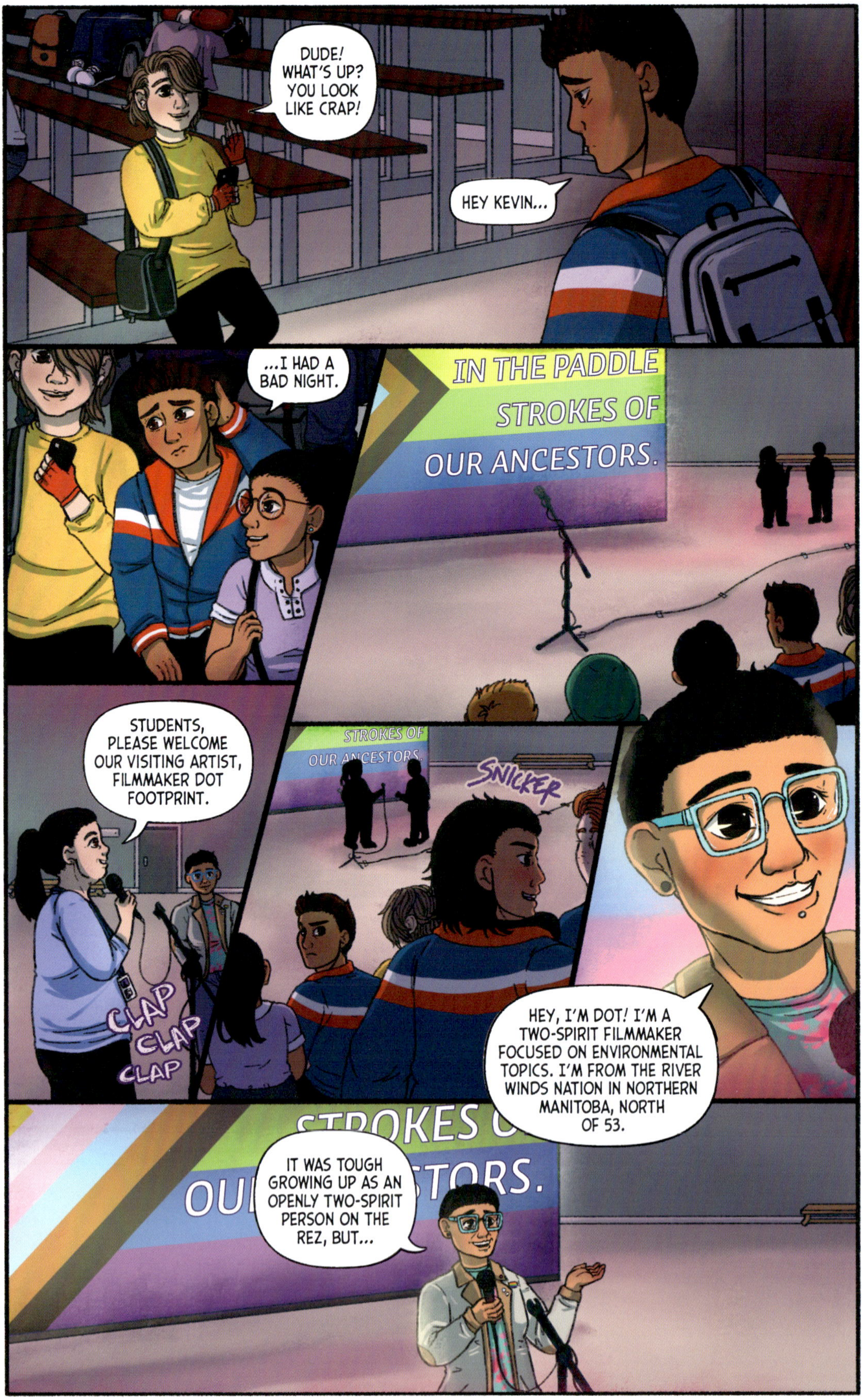
DUDE! WHAT'S UP? YOU LOOK LIKE CRAP!
HEY KEVIN...
...I HAD A BAD NIGHT.
IN THE PADDLE STROKES OF OUR ANCESTORS.
STUDENTS, PLEASE WELCOME OUR VISITING ARTIST, FILMMAKER DOT FOOTPRINT.
CLAP CLAP CLAP
SNICKER
HEY, I'M DOT! I'M A TWO-SPIRIT FILMMAKER FOCUSED ON ENVIRONMENTAL TOPICS. I'M FROM THE RIVER WINDS NATION IN NORTHERN MANITOBA, NORTH OF 53.
IT WAS TOUGH GROWING UP AS AN OPENLY TWO-SPIRIT PERSON ON THE REZ, BUT...

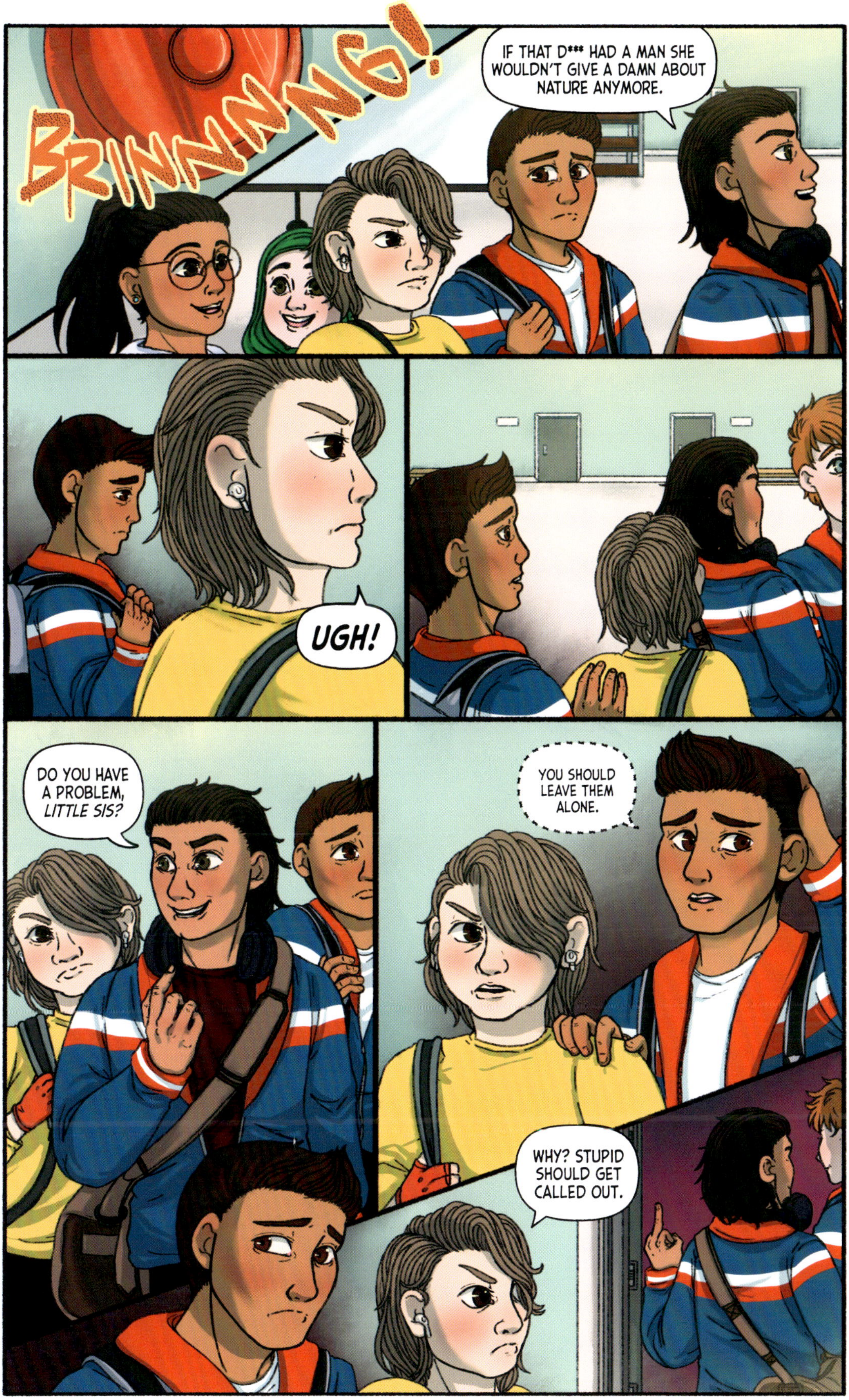
BRINNNNG!
IF THAT D*** HAD A MAN SHE WOULDN'T GIVE A DAMN ABOUT NATURE ANYMORE.
UGH!
DO YOU HAVE A PROBLEM, *LITTLE SIS?*
YOU SHOULD LEAVE THEM ALONE.
WHY? STUPID SHOULD GET CALLED OUT.

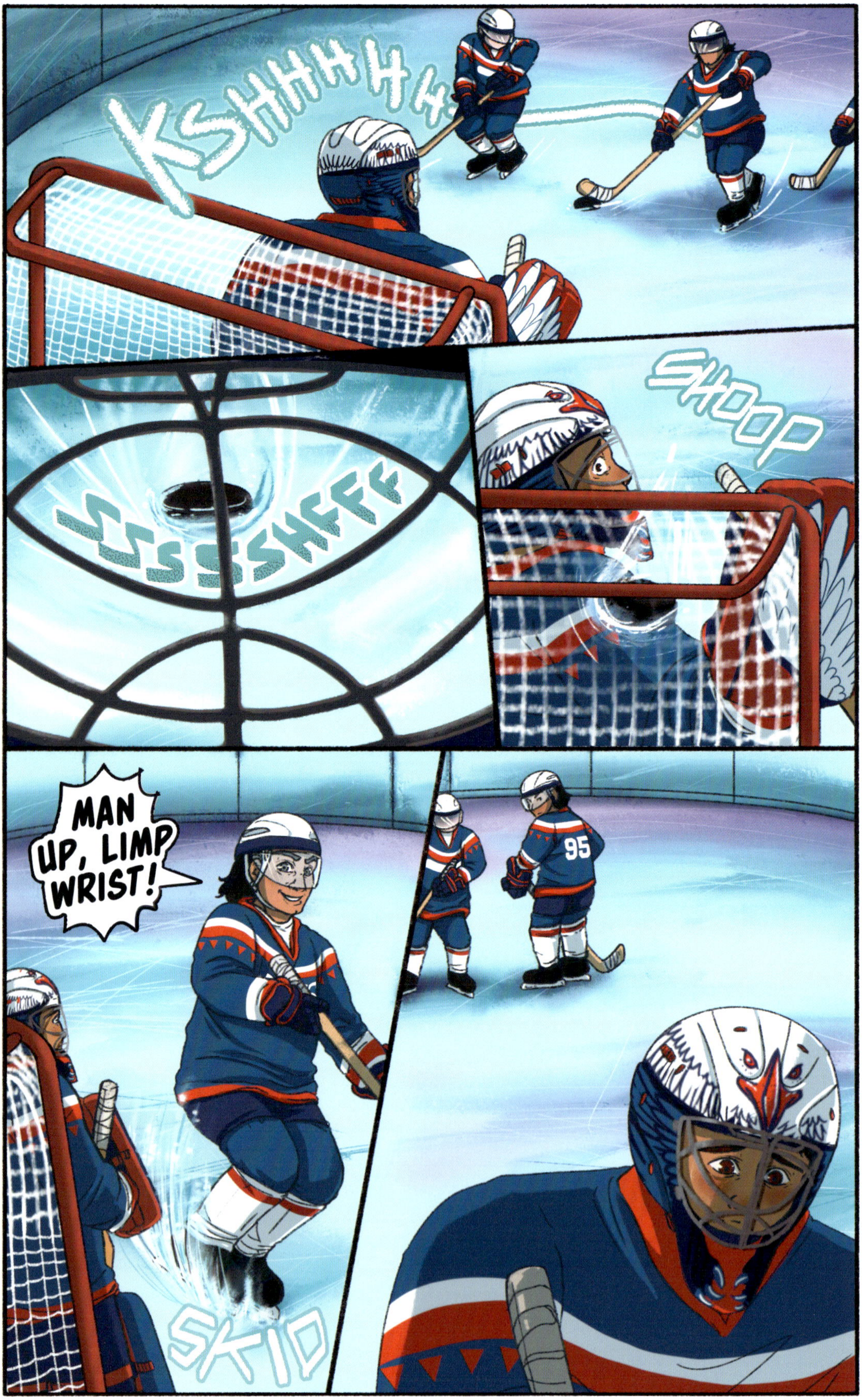
KSHHHHH
SSSSHFFF
SHOOP
MAN UP, LIMP WRIST!
SKID
95

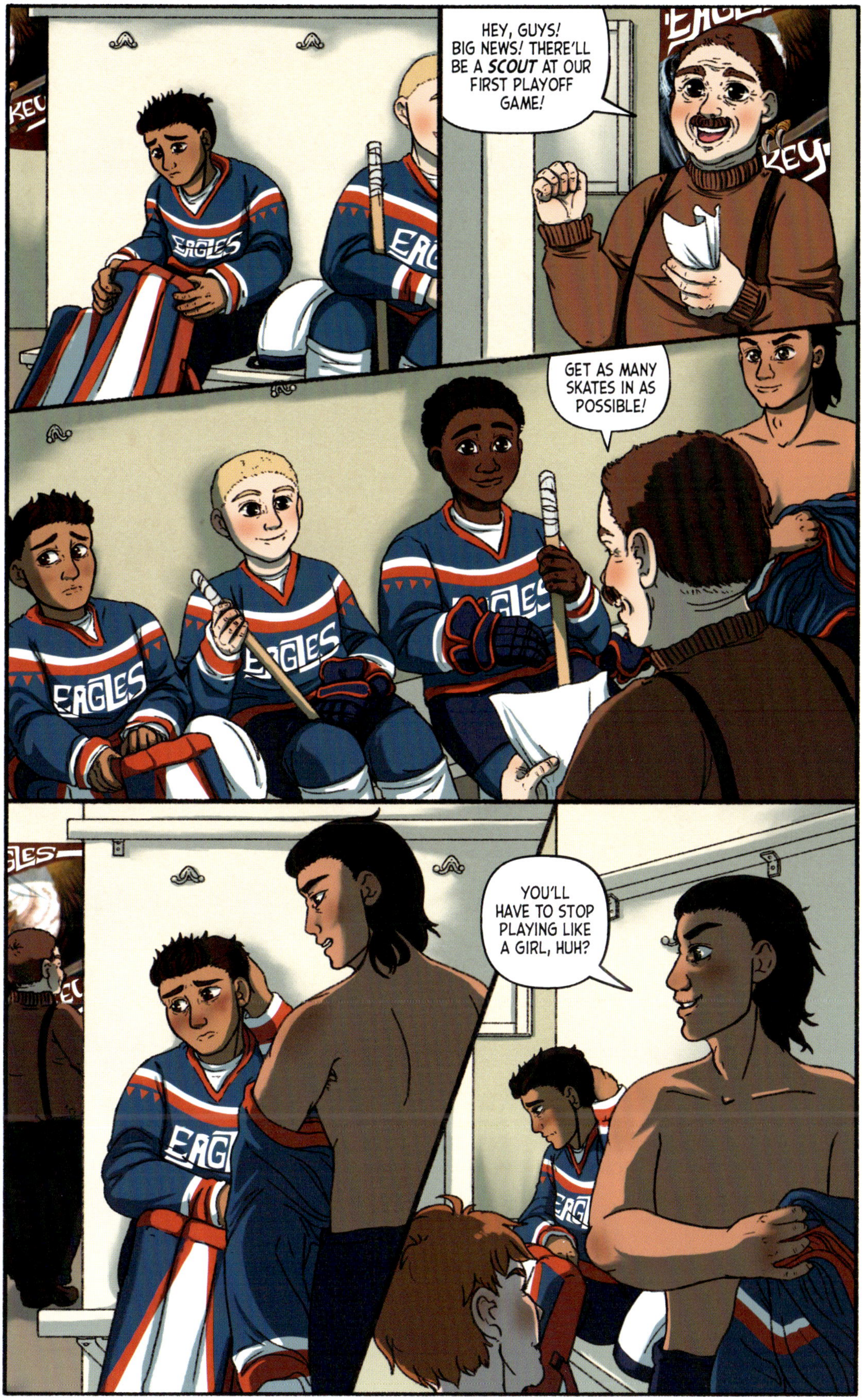
HEY, GUYS! BIG NEWS! THERE'LL BE A **SCOUT** AT OUR FIRST PLAYOFF GAME!
GET AS MANY SKATES IN AS POSSIBLE!
YOU'LL HAVE TO STOP PLAYING LIKE A GIRL, HUH?

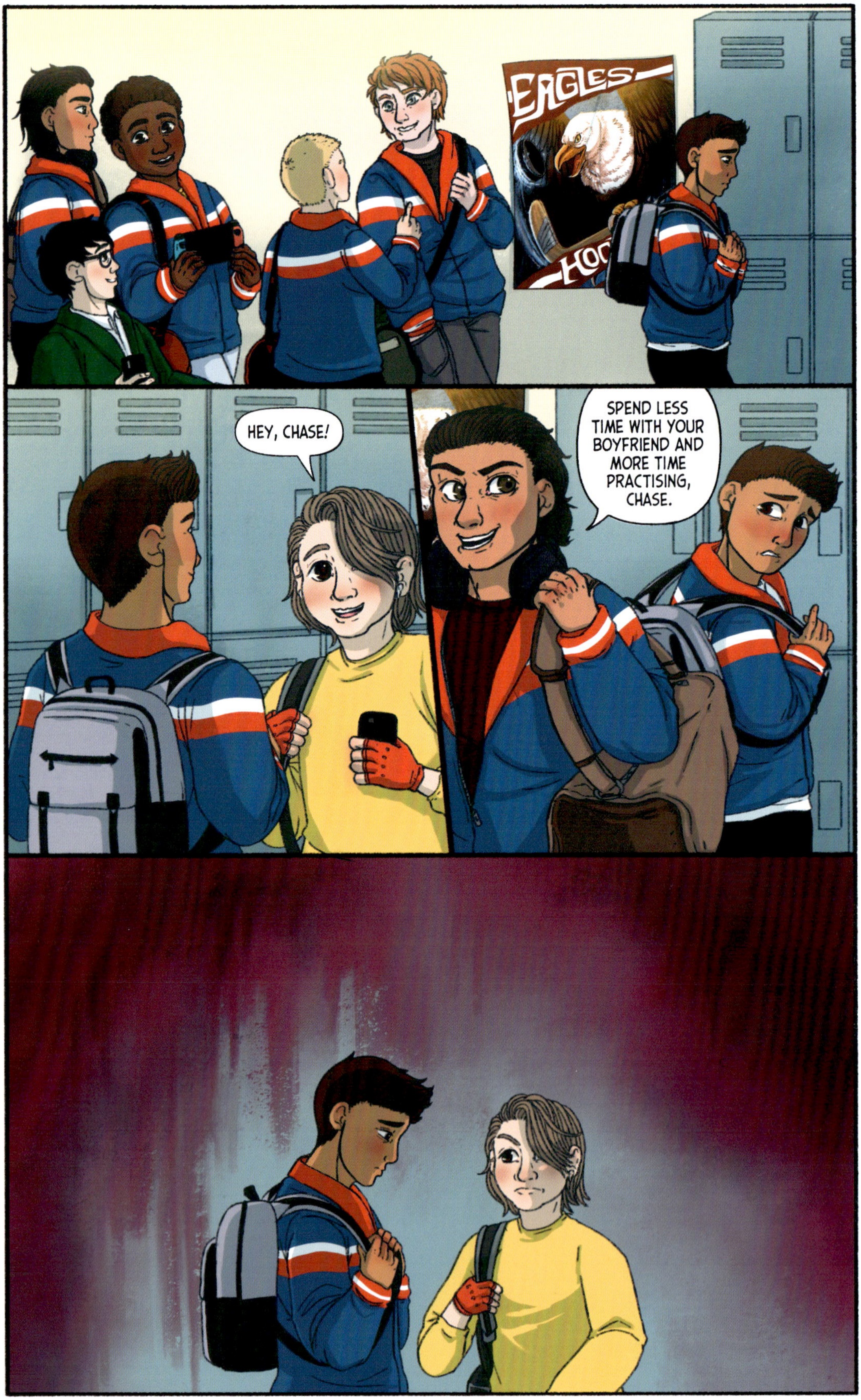
EAGLES
HOC
HEY, CHASE!
SPEND LESS TIME WITH YOUR BOYFRIEND AND MORE TIME PRACTISING, CHASE.

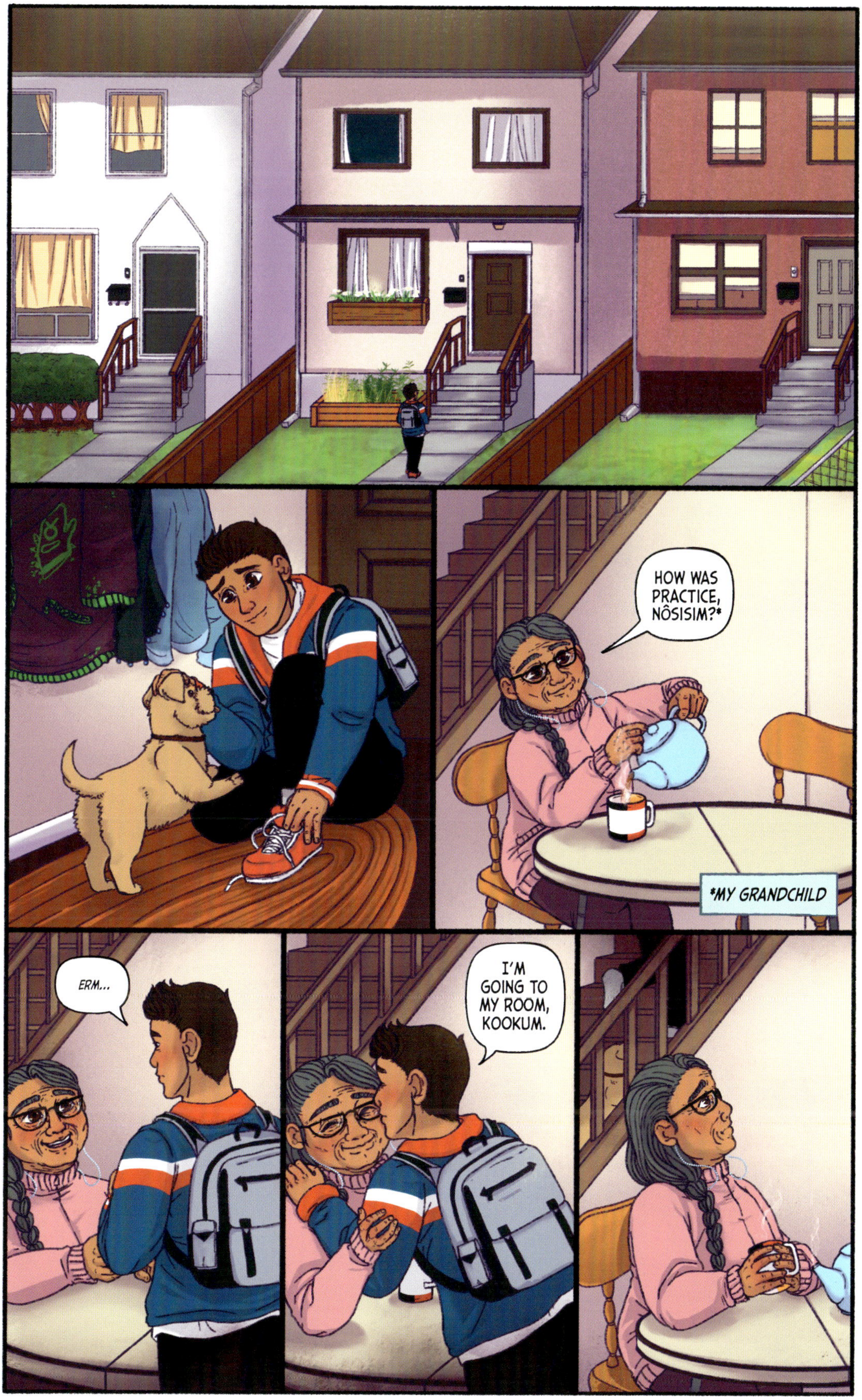
HOW WAS PRACTICE, NÔSISIM?*
*MY GRANDCHILD
ERM...
I'M GOING TO MY ROOM, KOOKUM.

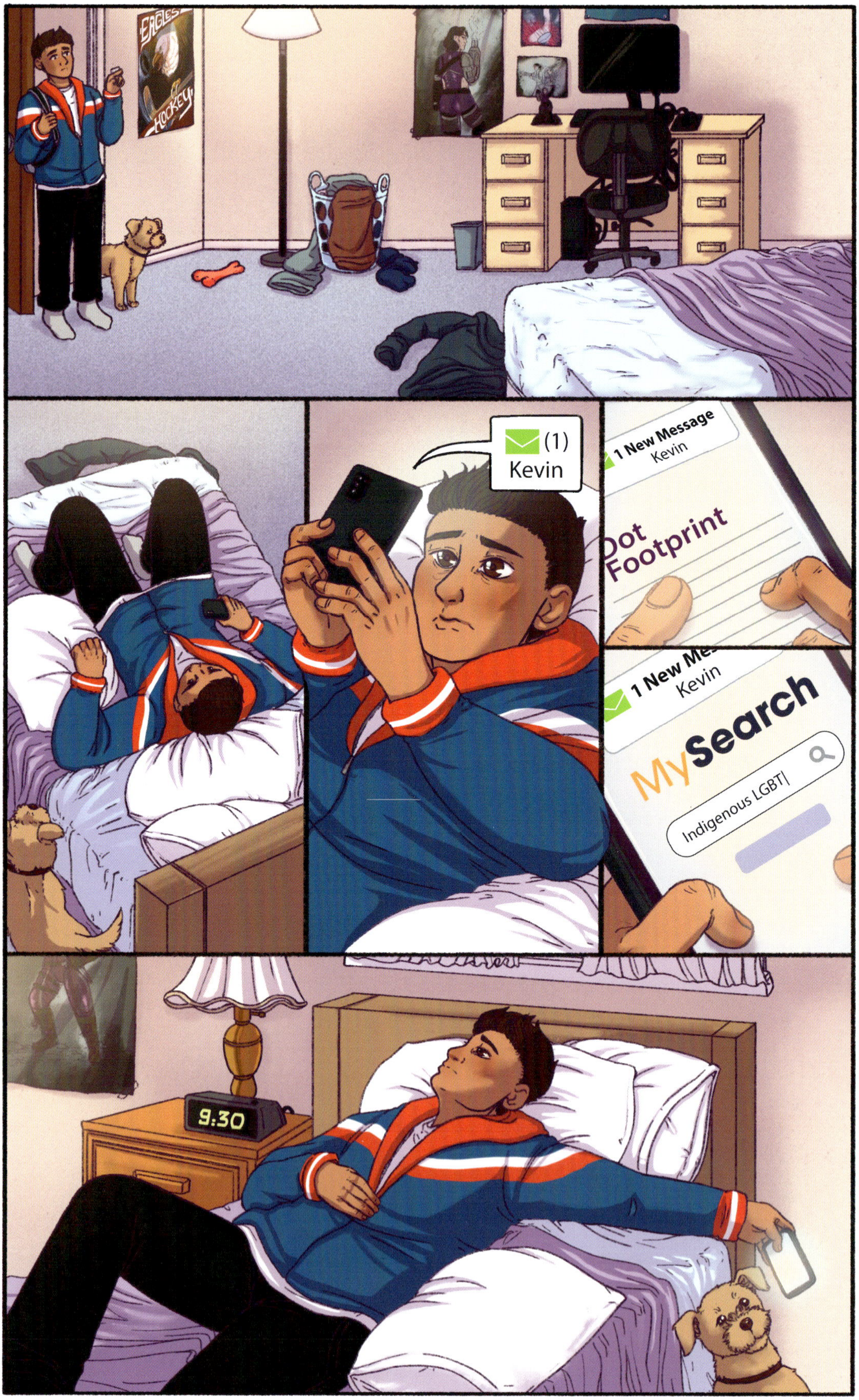
EAGLES
HOCKEY
(1)
Kevin
1 New Message
Kevin
Dot
Footprint
Kevin
MySearch
Indigenous LGBT|
9:30

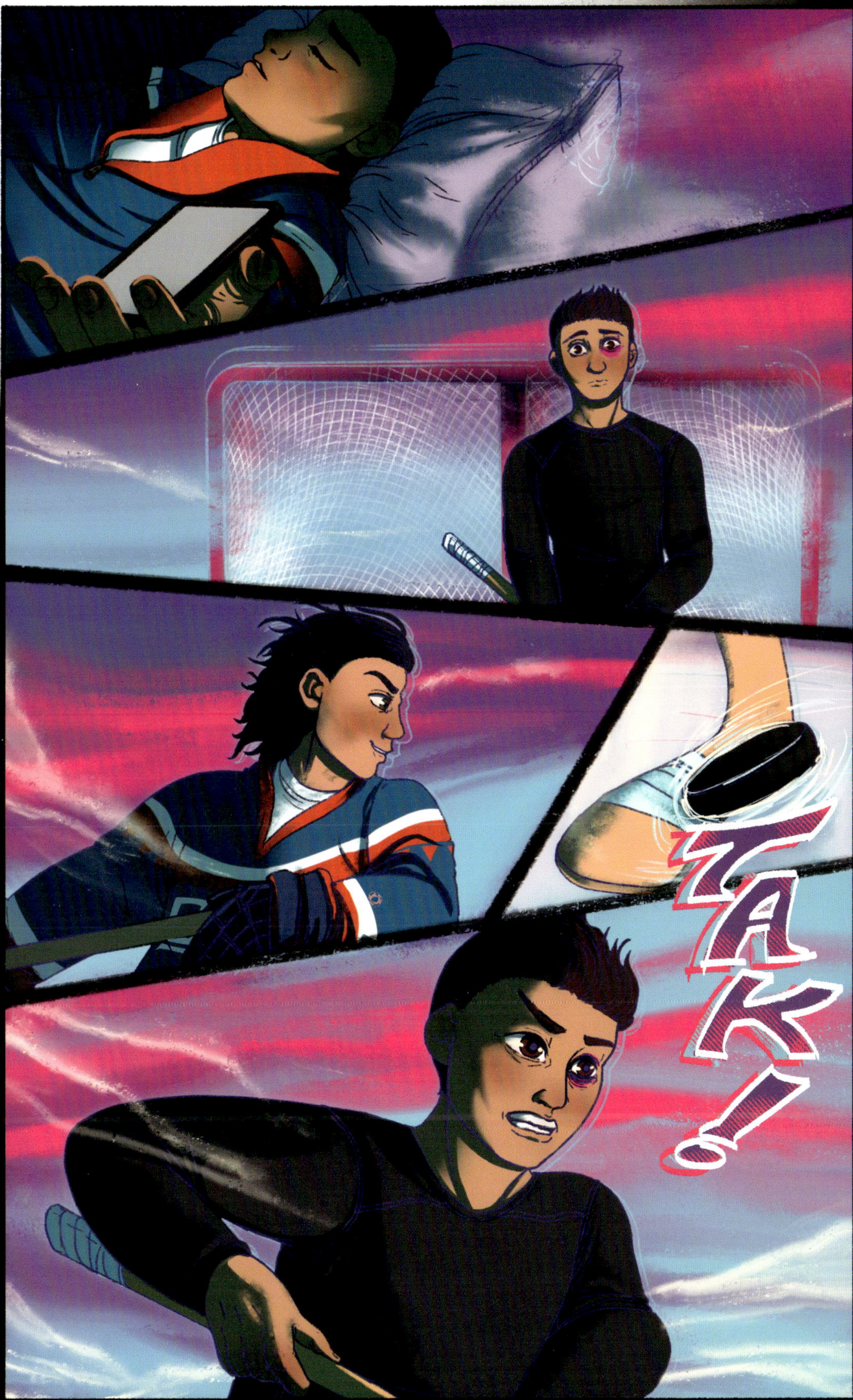
TAK!

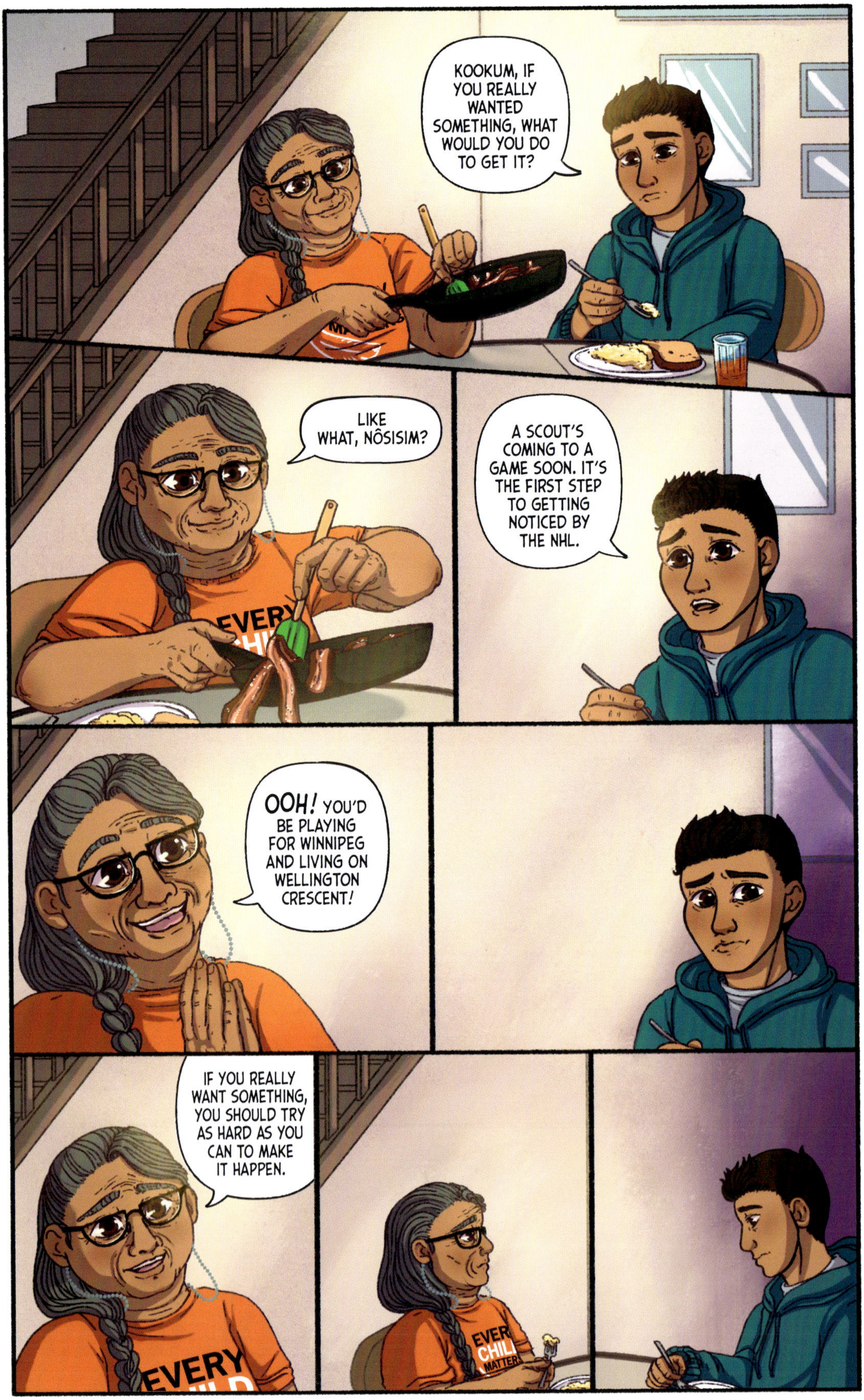
KOOKUM, IF YOU REALLY WANTED SOMETHING, WHAT WOULD YOU DO TO GET IT?
LIKE WHAT, NÔSISIM?
A SCOUT'S COMING TO A GAME SOON. IT'S THE FIRST STEP TO GETTING NOTICED BY THE NHL.
OOH! YOU'D BE PLAYING FOR WINNIPEG AND LIVING ON WELLINGTON CRESCENT!
IF YOU REALLY WANT SOMETHING, YOU SHOULD TRY AS HARD AS YOU CAN TO MAKE IT HAPPEN.

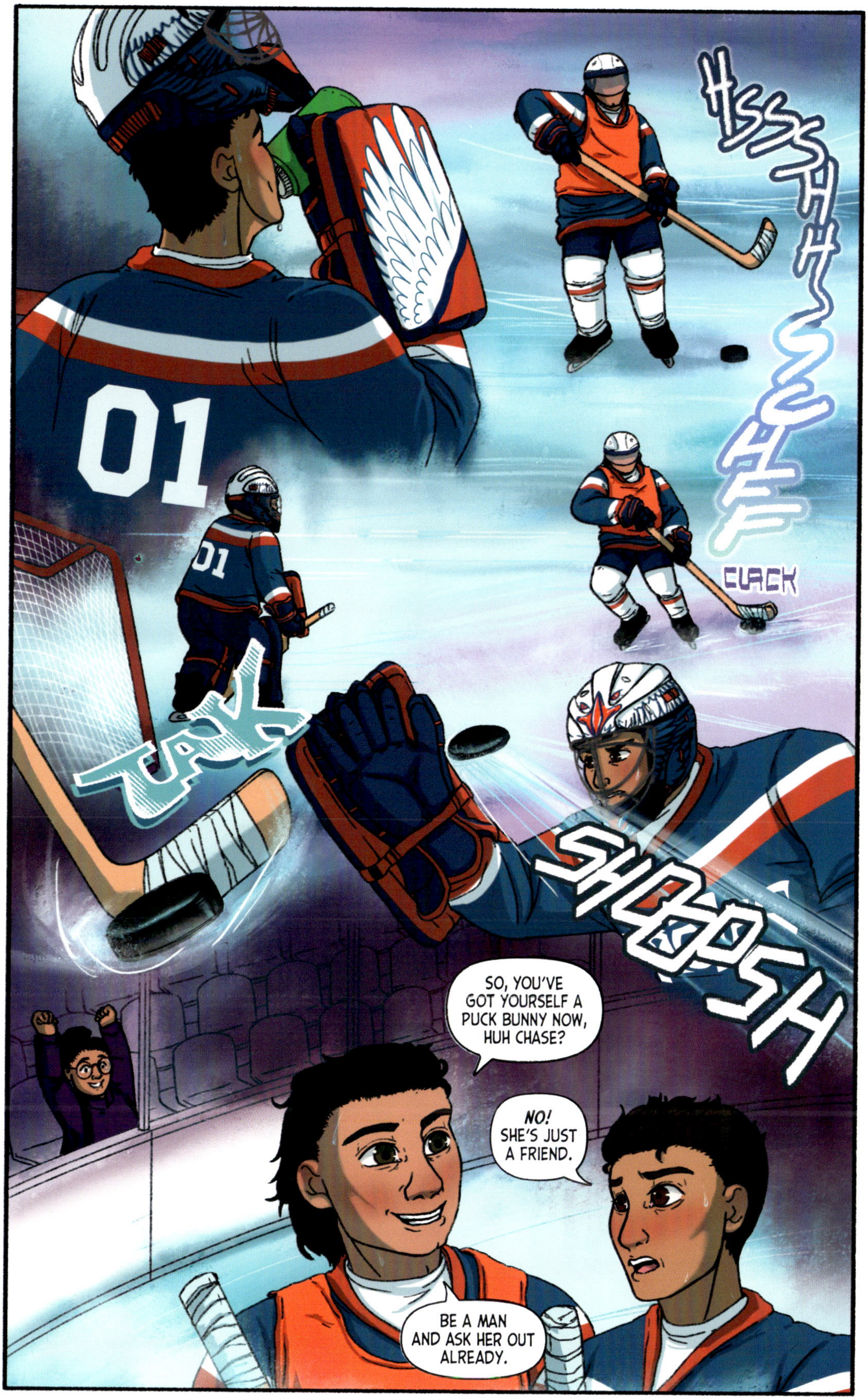
HSSSHH—SCHFF
CLACK
TAK
SHOOSH
SO, YOU'VE GOT YOURSELF A PUCK BUNNY NOW, HUH CHASE?
NO! SHE'S JUST A FRIEND.
BE A MAN AND ASK HER OUT ALREADY.

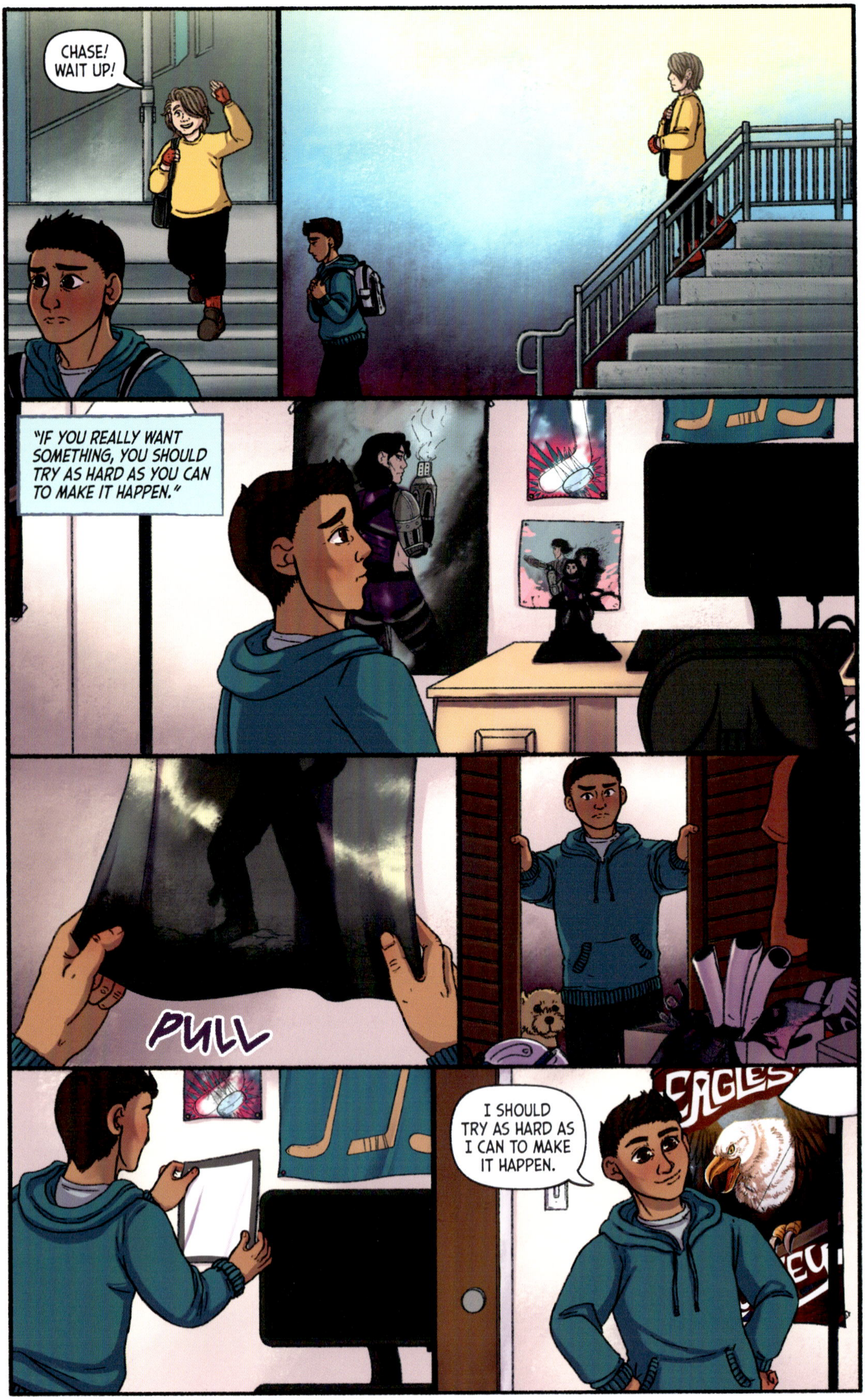
CHASE! WAIT UP!
"IF YOU REALLY WANT SOMETHING, YOU SHOULD TRY AS HARD AS YOU CAN TO MAKE IT HAPPEN."
PULL
I SHOULD TRY AS HARD AS I CAN TO MAKE IT HAPPEN.
EAGLES

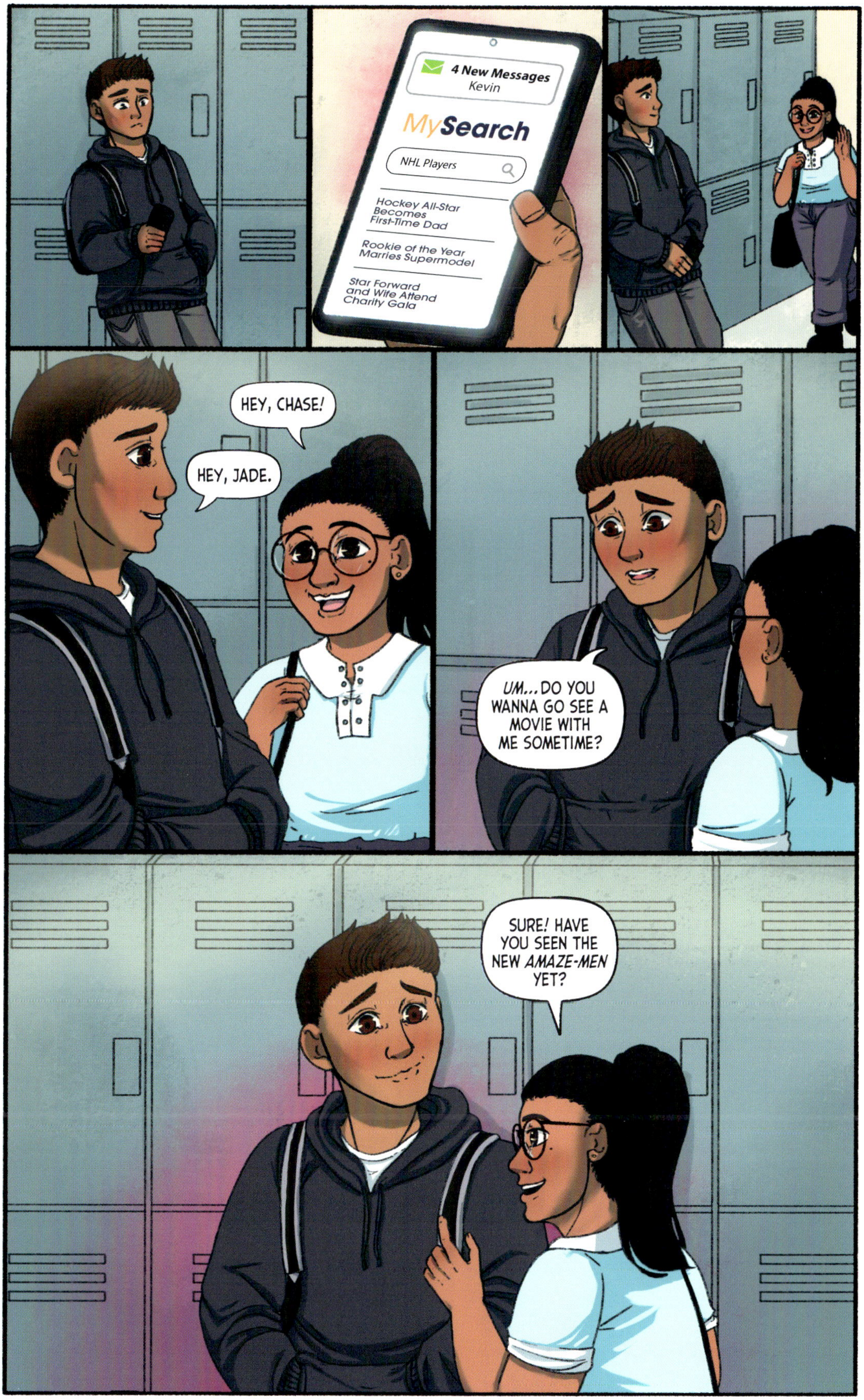
4 New Messages
Kevin
MySearch
NHL Players
Hockey All-Star Becomes First-Time Dad
Rookie of the Year Marries Supermodel
Star Forward and Wife Attend Charity Gala
HEY, CHASE!
HEY, JADE.
UM... DO YOU WANNA GO SEE A MOVIE WITH ME SOMETIME?
SURE! HAVE YOU SEEN THE NEW *AMAZE-MEN* YET?

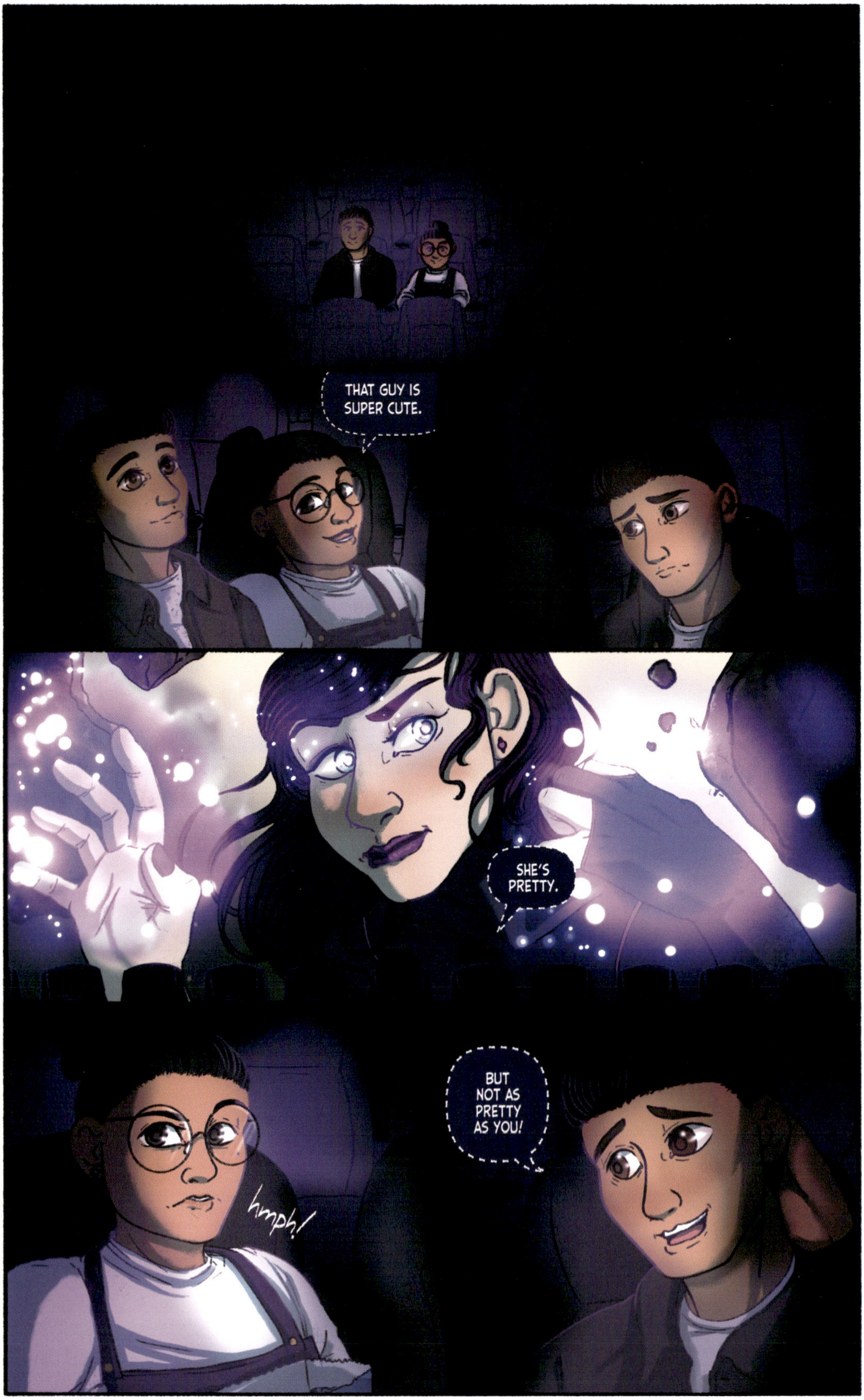
THAT GUY IS SUPER CUTE.
SHE'S PRETTY.
BUT NOT AS PRETTY AS YOU!
hmph!

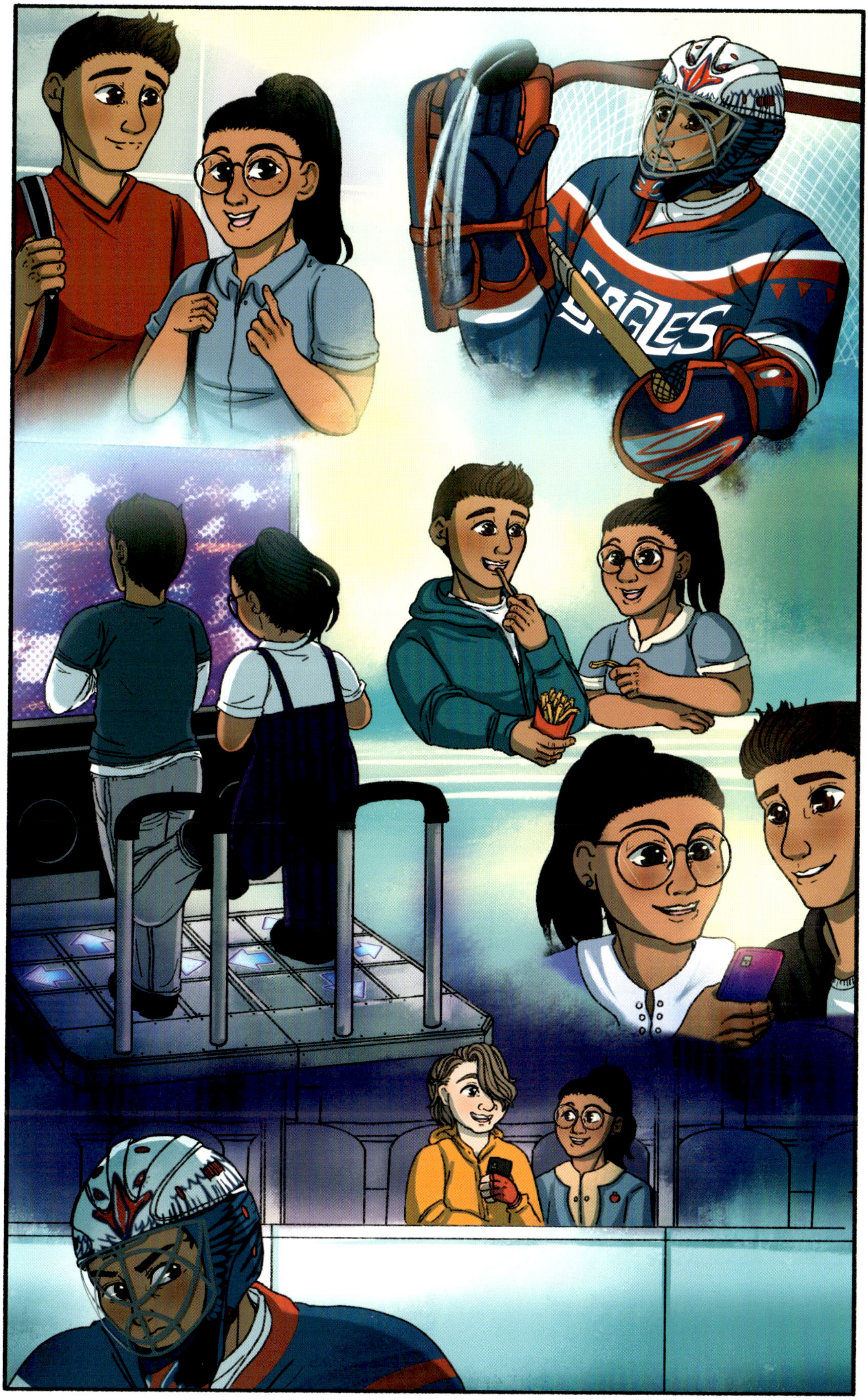
EAGLES

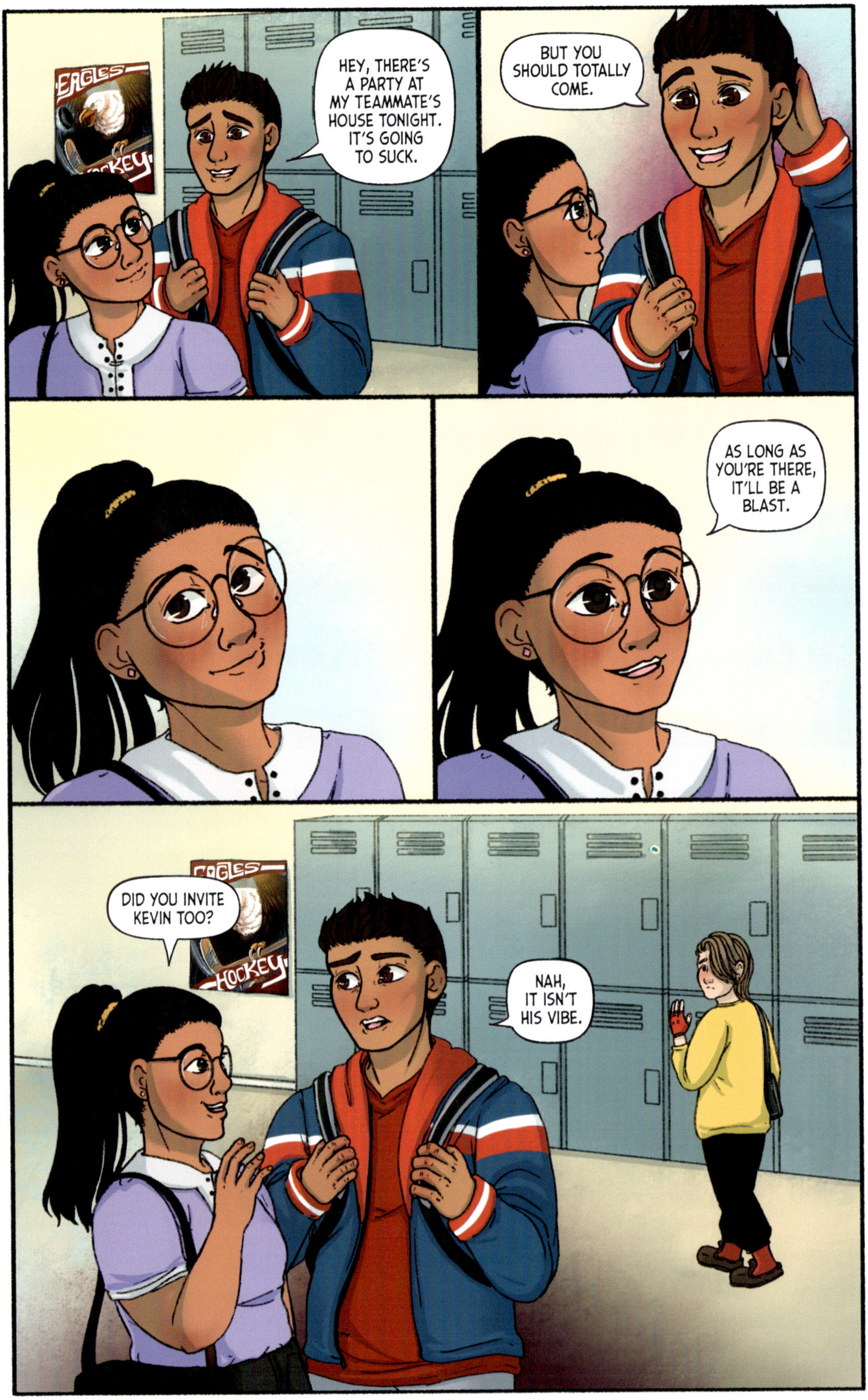
EAGLES
HOCKEY
HEY, THERE'S A PARTY AT MY TEAMMATE'S HOUSE TONIGHT. IT'S GOING TO SUCK.
BUT YOU SHOULD TOTALLY COME.
AS LONG AS YOU'RE THERE, IT'LL BE A BLAST.
DID YOU INVITE KEVIN TOO?
NAH, IT ISN'T HIS VIBE.

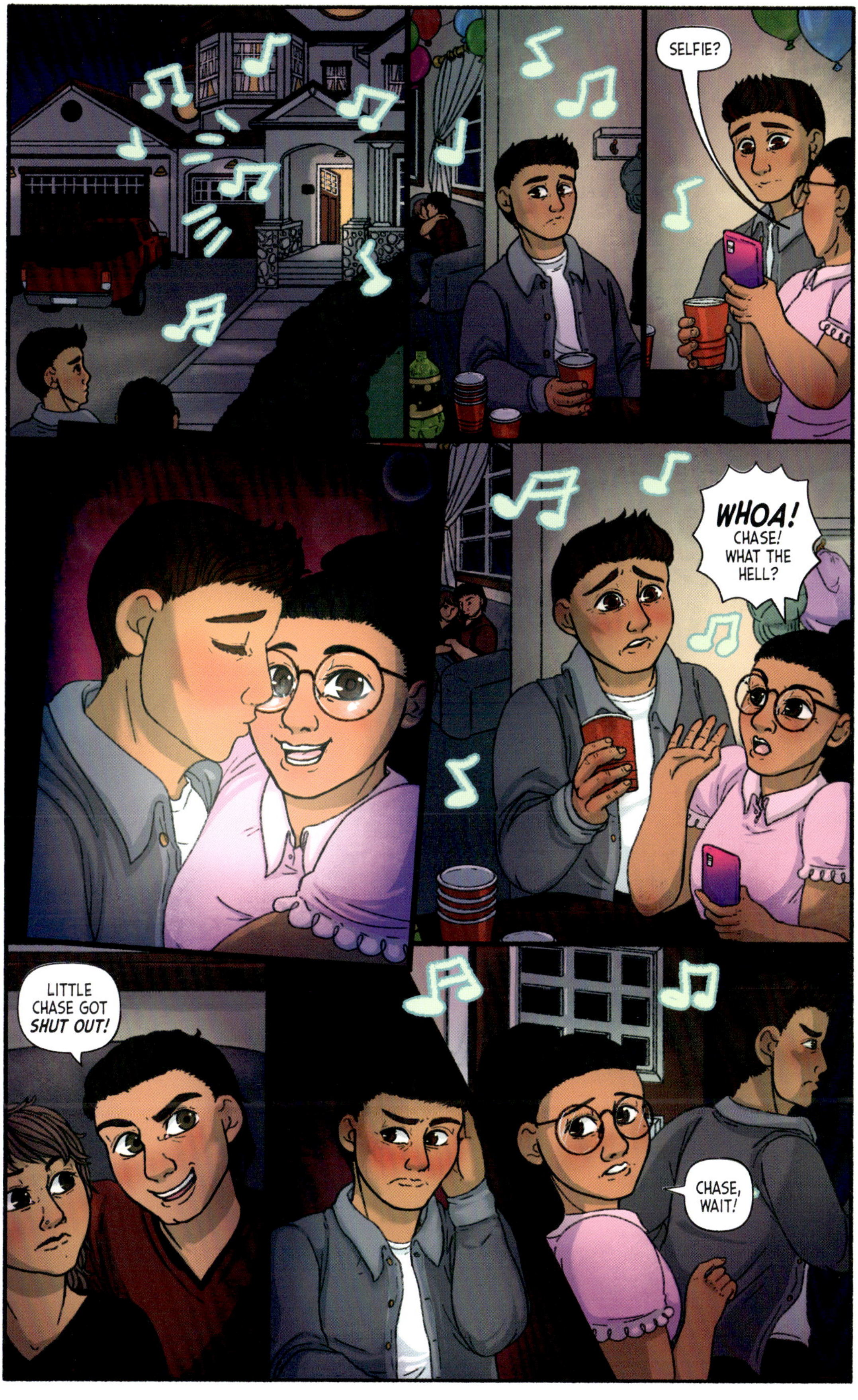
SELFIE?
WHOA! CHASE! WHAT THE HELL?
LITTLE CHASE GOT SHUT OUT!
CHASE, WAIT!

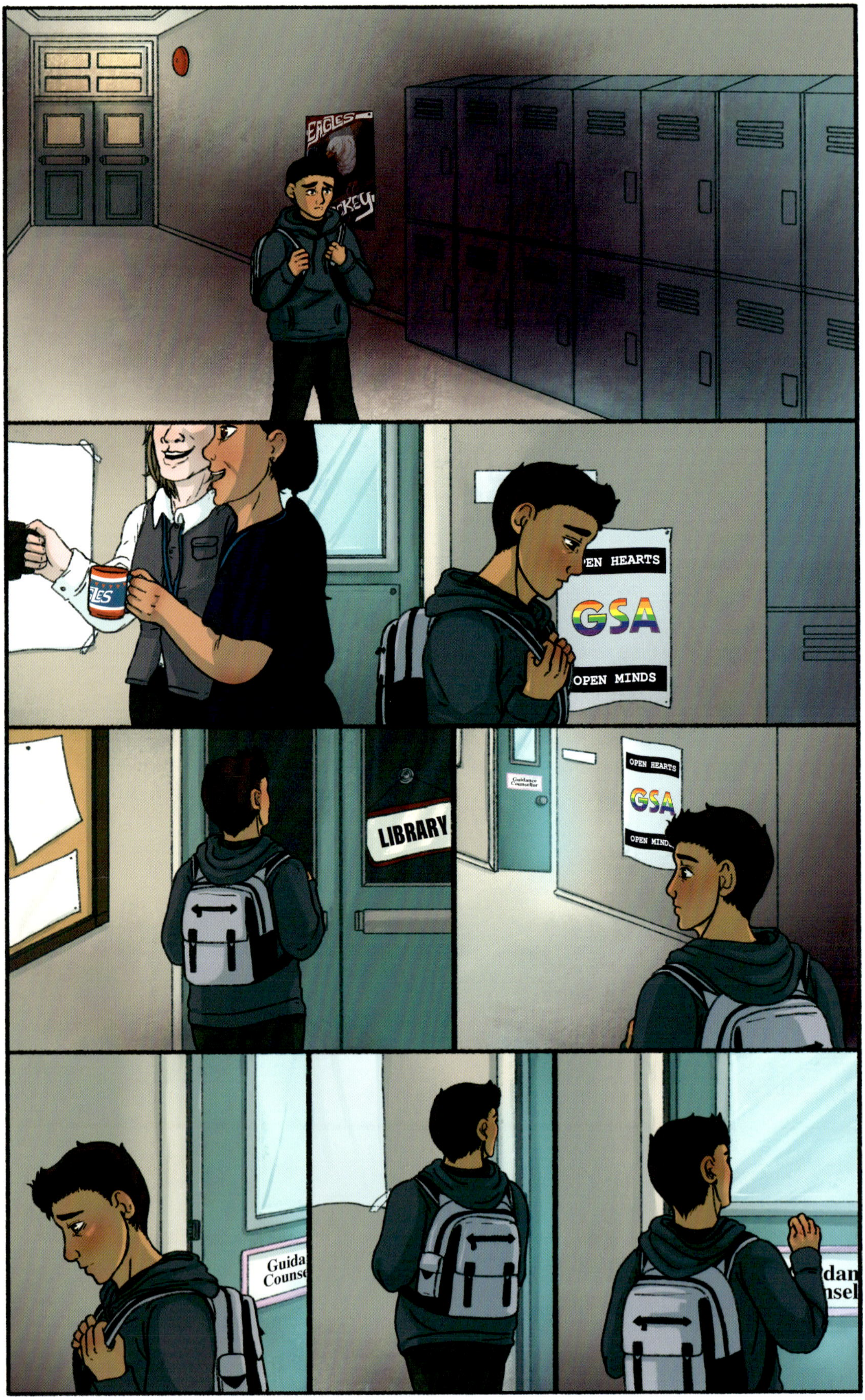
EAGLES
OPEN HEARTS
GSA
OPEN MINDS
LIBRARY
Guidance Counsellor

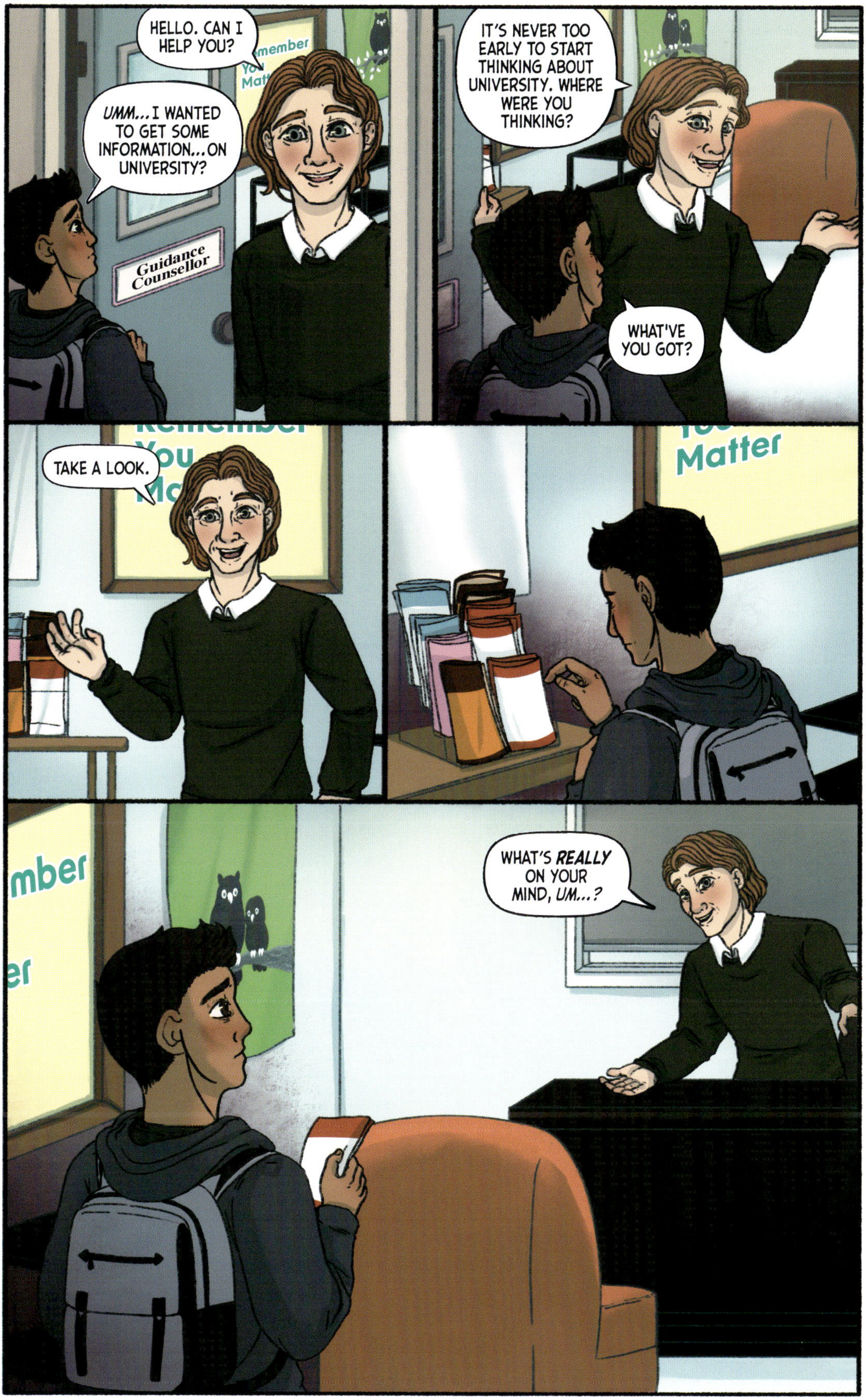
HELLO. CAN I HELP YOU?
UMM... I WANTED TO GET SOME INFORMATION... ON UNIVERSITY?
Guidance Counsellor
IT'S NEVER TOO EARLY TO START THINKING ABOUT UNIVERSITY. WHERE WERE YOU THINKING?
WHAT'VE YOU GOT?
TAKE A LOOK.
Matter
WHAT'S REALLY ON YOUR MIND, UM...?

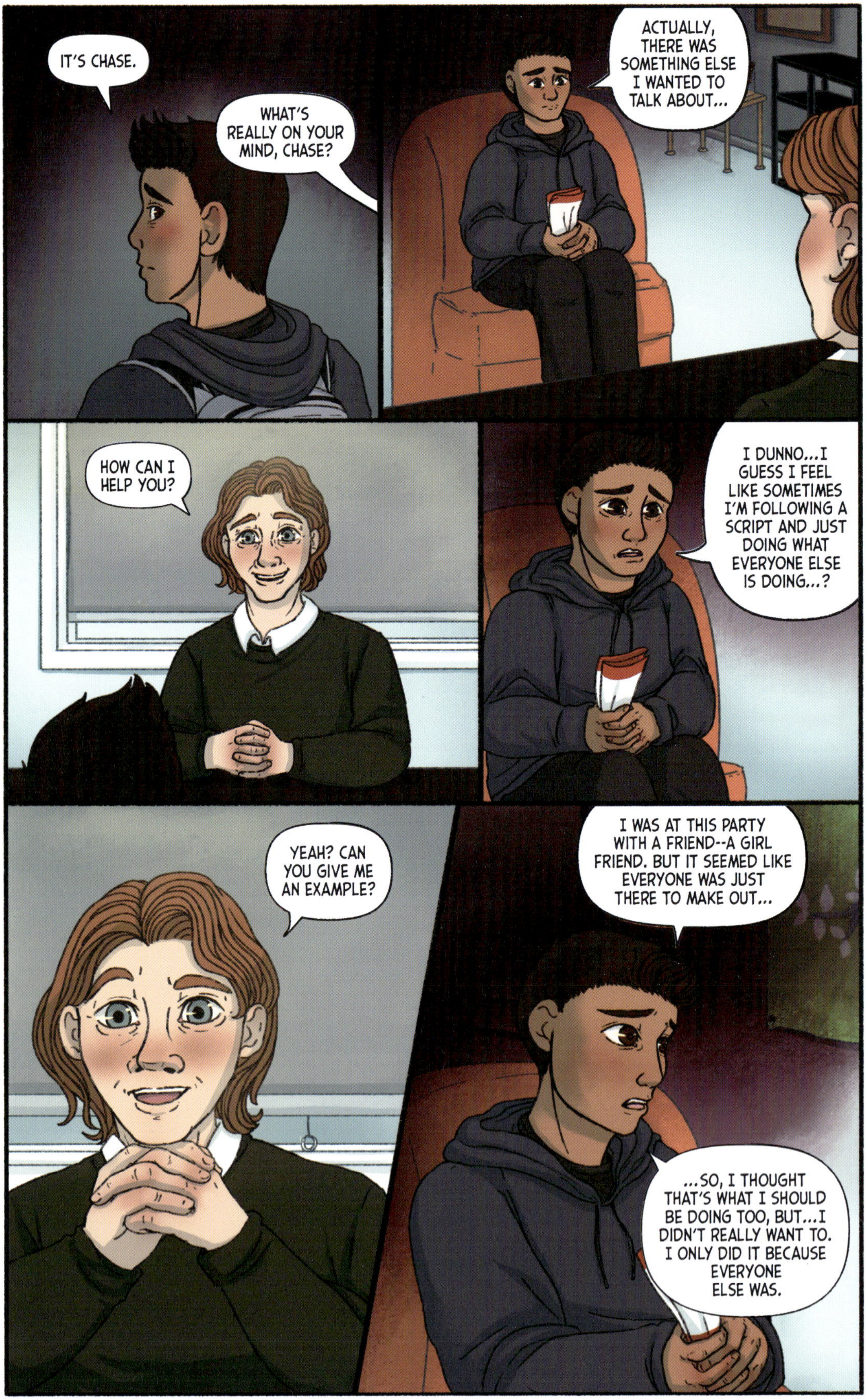
IT'S CHASE.
WHAT'S REALLY ON YOUR MIND, CHASE?
ACTUALLY, THERE WAS SOMETHING ELSE I WANTED TO TALK ABOUT...
HOW CAN I HELP YOU?
I DUNNO...I GUESS I FEEL LIKE SOMETIMES I'M FOLLOWING A SCRIPT AND JUST DOING WHAT EVERYONE ELSE IS DOING...?
YEAH? CAN YOU GIVE ME AN EXAMPLE?
I WAS AT THIS PARTY WITH A FRIEND--A GIRL FRIEND. BUT IT SEEMED LIKE EVERYONE WAS JUST THERE TO MAKE OUT...
...SO, I THOUGHT THAT'S WHAT I SHOULD BE DOING TOO, BUT...I DIDN'T REALLY WANT TO. I ONLY DID IT BECAUSE EVERYONE ELSE WAS.

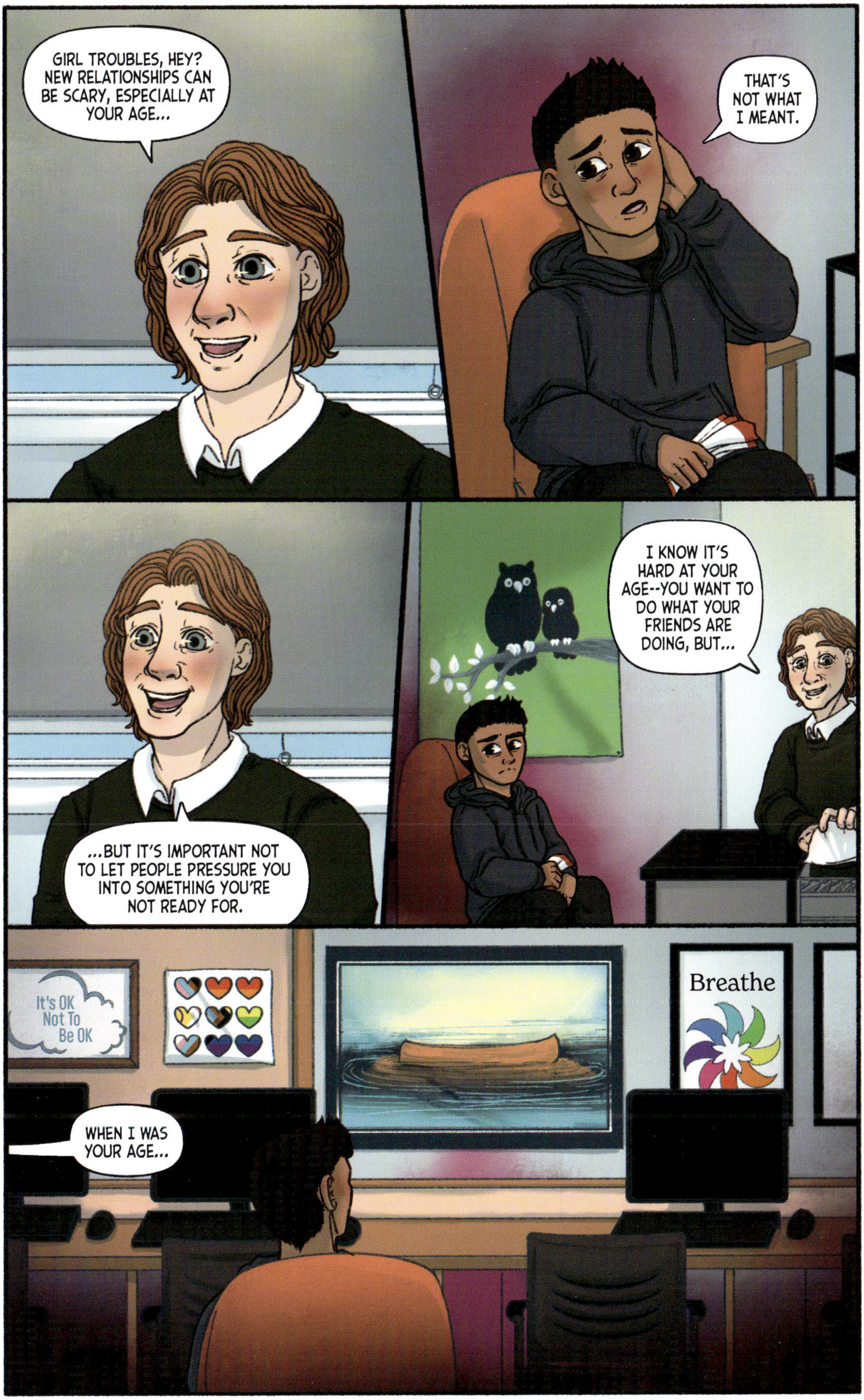
GIRL TROUBLES, HEY? NEW RELATIONSHIPS CAN BE SCARY, ESPECIALLY AT YOUR AGE...
THAT'S NOT WHAT I MEANT.
...BUT IT'S IMPORTANT NOT TO LET PEOPLE PRESSURE YOU INTO SOMETHING YOU'RE NOT READY FOR.
I KNOW IT'S HARD AT YOUR AGE--YOU WANT TO DO WHAT YOUR FRIENDS ARE DOING, BUT...
It's OK Not To Be OK
Breathe
WHEN I WAS YOUR AGE...

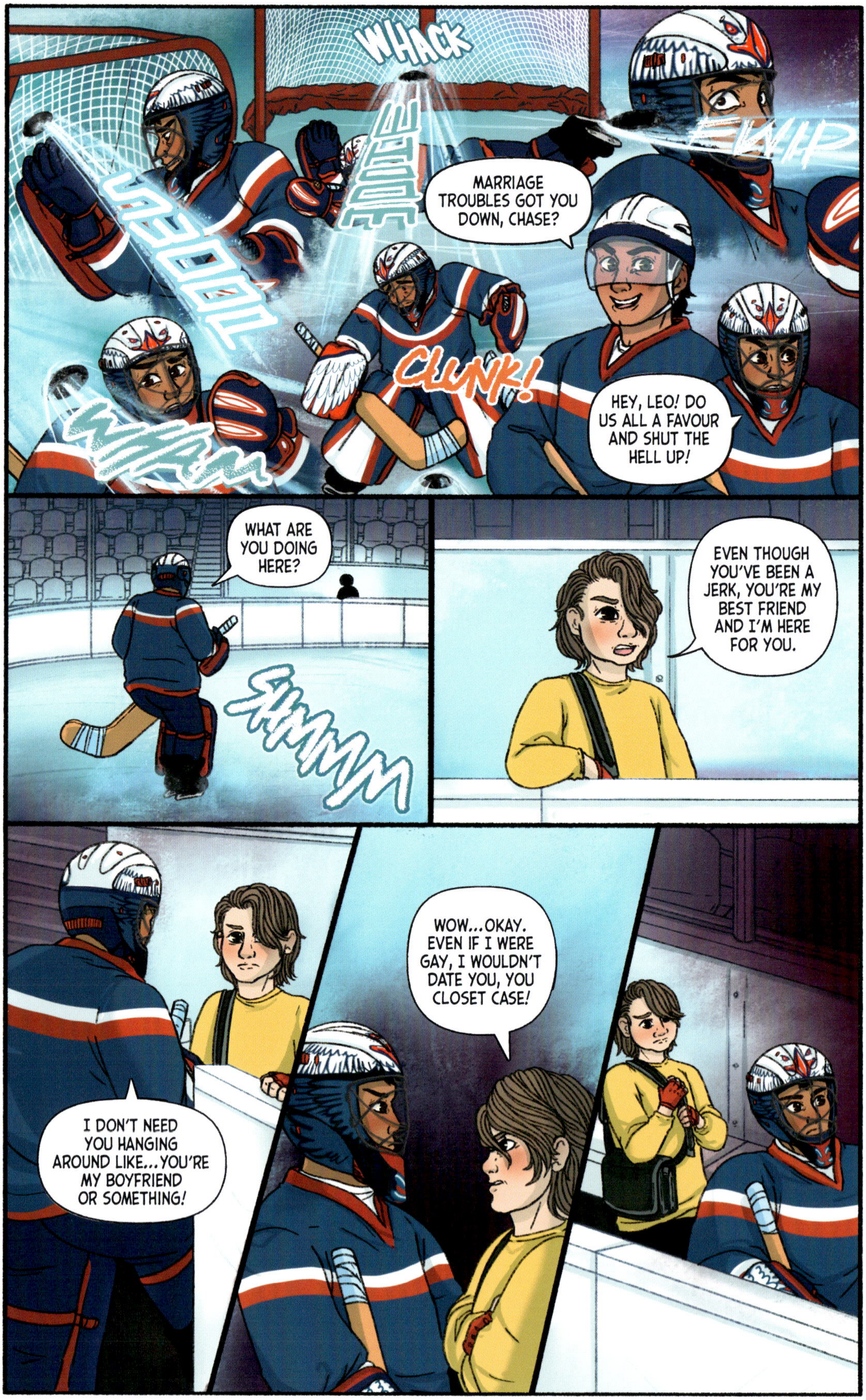
WHACK
THWIP
FWIP
DOOSH
MARRIAGE TROUBLES GOT YOU DOWN, CHASE?
CLUNK!
WHAM
HEY, LEO! DO US ALL A FAVOUR AND SHUT THE HELL UP!
WHAT ARE YOU DOING HERE?
SHHHHH
EVEN THOUGH YOU'VE BEEN A JERK, YOU'RE MY BEST FRIEND AND I'M HERE FOR YOU.
I DON'T NEED YOU HANGING AROUND LIKE...YOU'RE MY BOYFRIEND OR SOMETHING!
WOW...OKAY. EVEN IF I WERE GAY, I WOULDN'T DATE YOU, YOU CLOSET CASE!

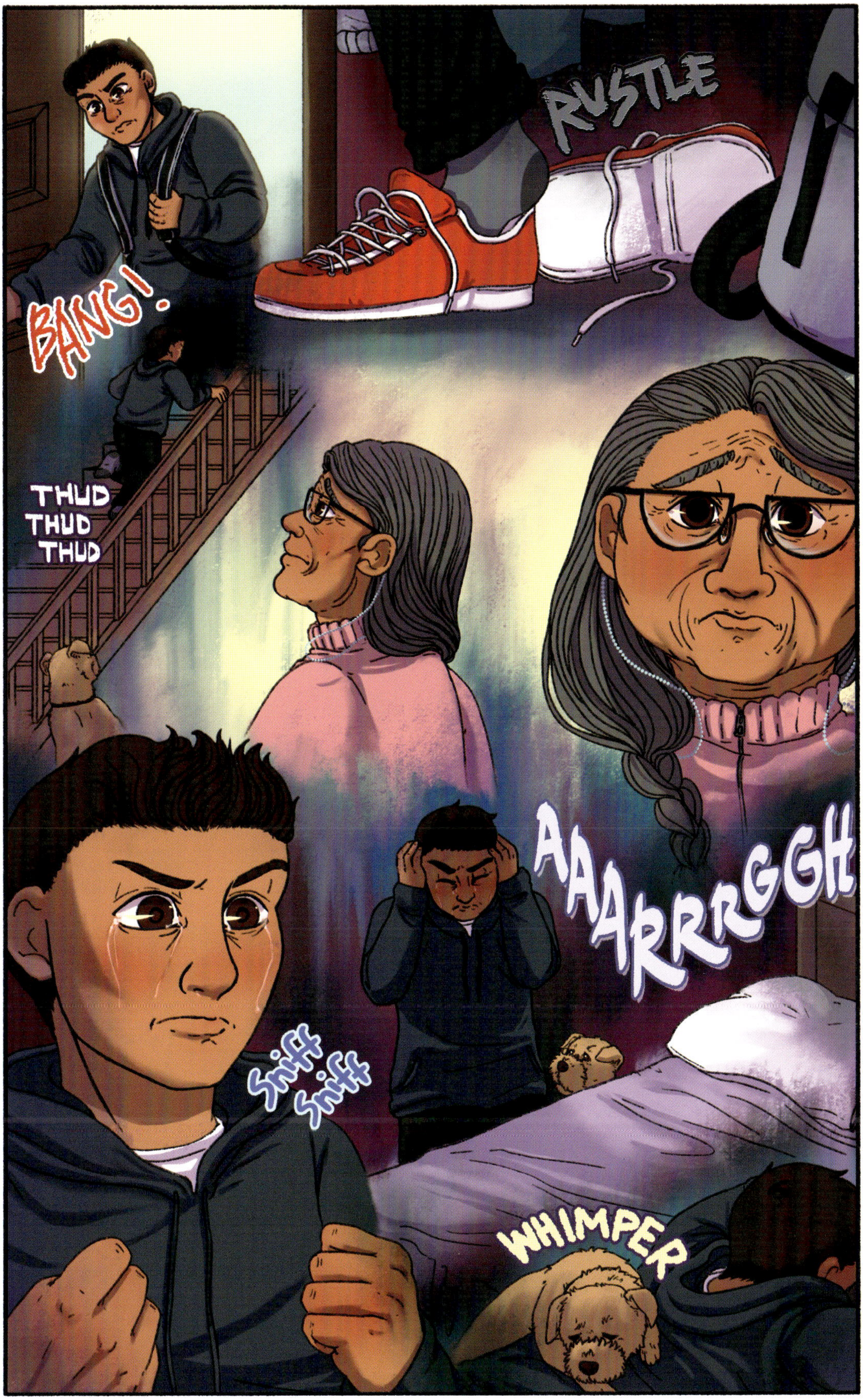
RUSTLE
BANG!
THUD
THUD
THUD
AAARRRGGH
Sniff
Sniff
WHIMPER

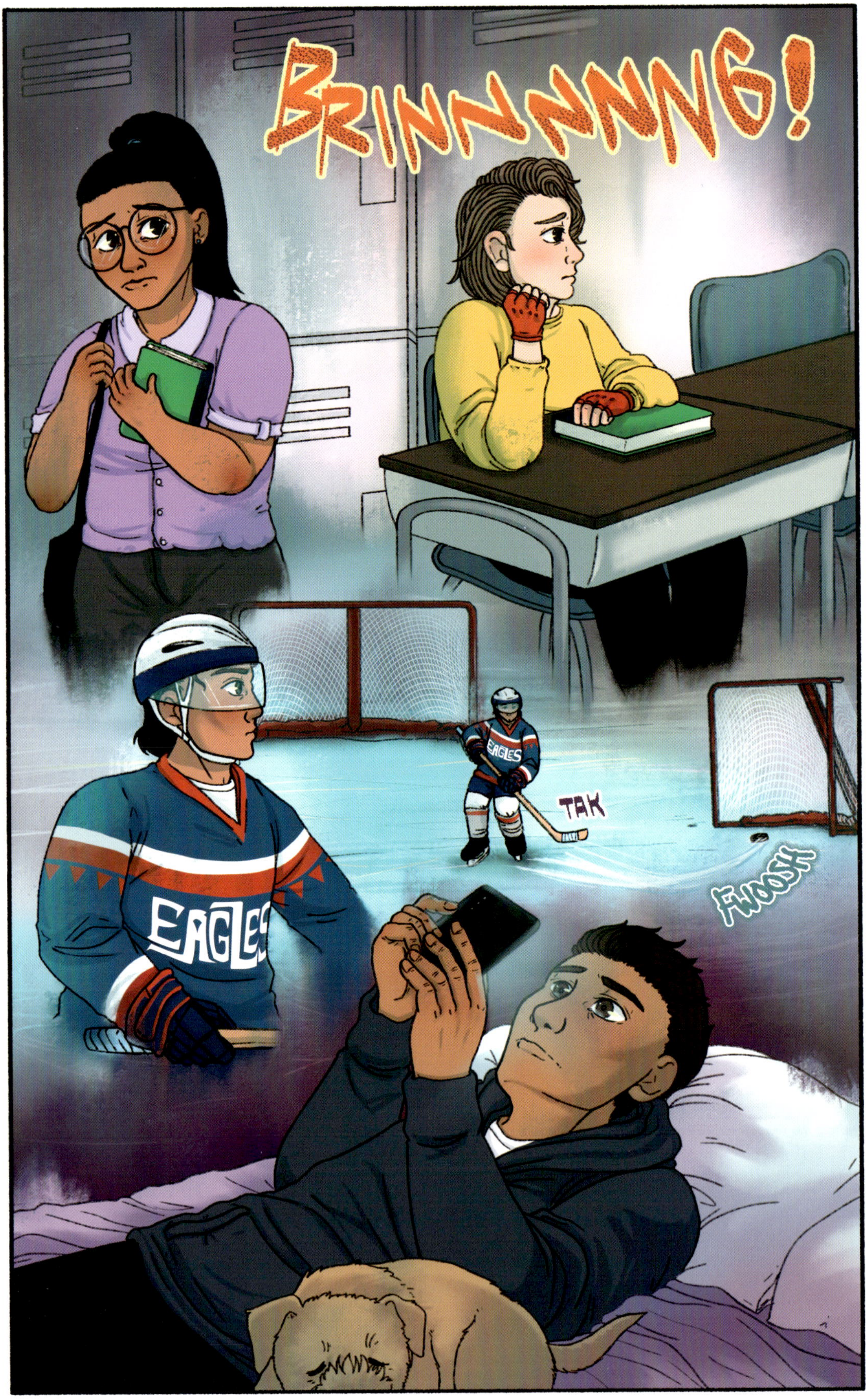
BRINNNNNG!
EAGLES
TAK
FWOOSH
EAGLES

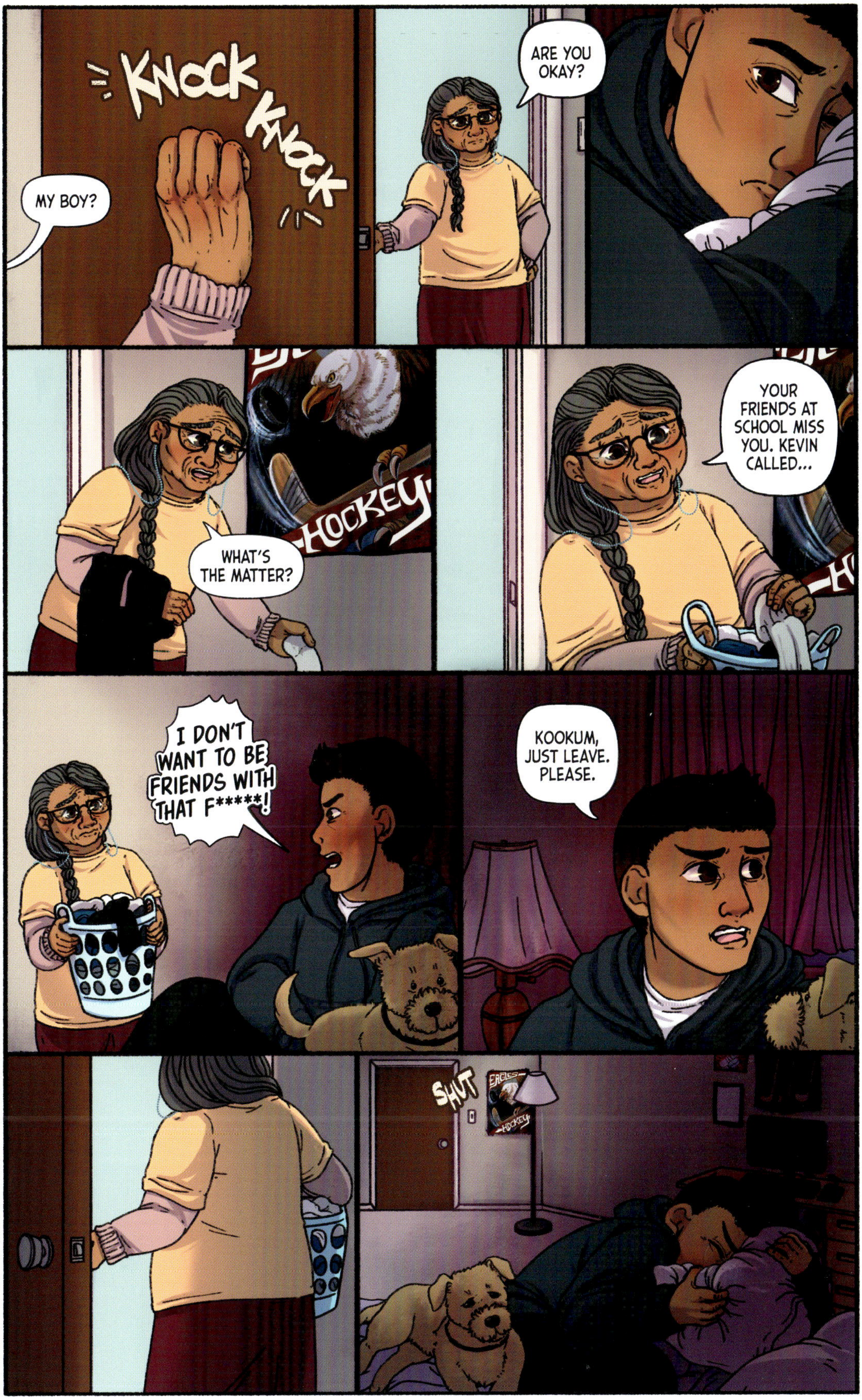

KNOCK KNOCK
MY BOY?
ARE YOU OKAY?
WHAT'S THE MATTER?
HOCKEY
YOUR FRIENDS AT SCHOOL MISS YOU. KEVIN CALLED...
I DON'T WANT TO BE FRIENDS WITH THAT F*****!
KOOKUM, JUST LEAVE. PLEASE.
SHUT

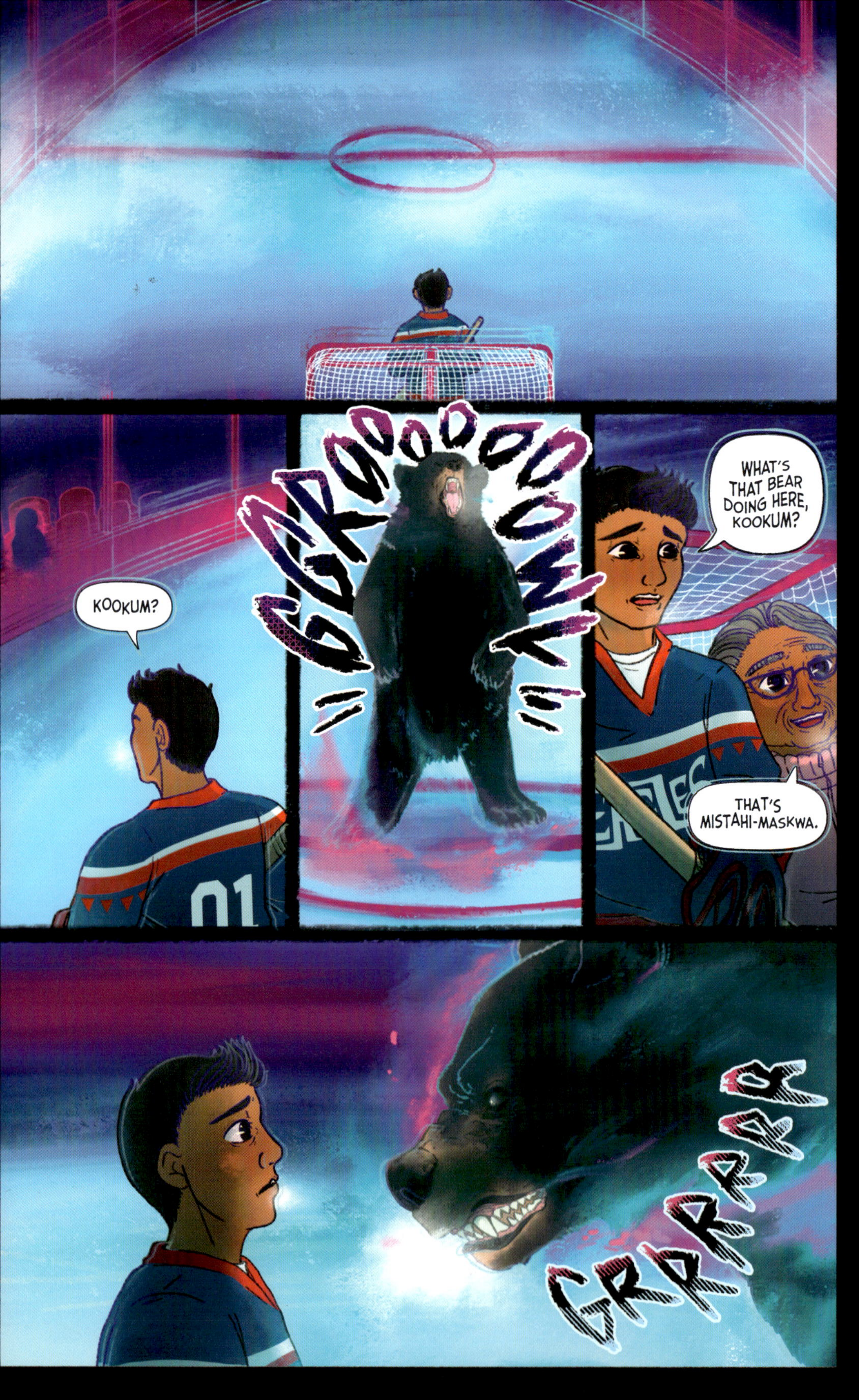
KOOKUM?
GGROOOOOOOWL
WHAT'S THAT BEAR DOING HERE, KOOKUM?
THAT'S MISTAHI-MASKWA.
GRRRRR

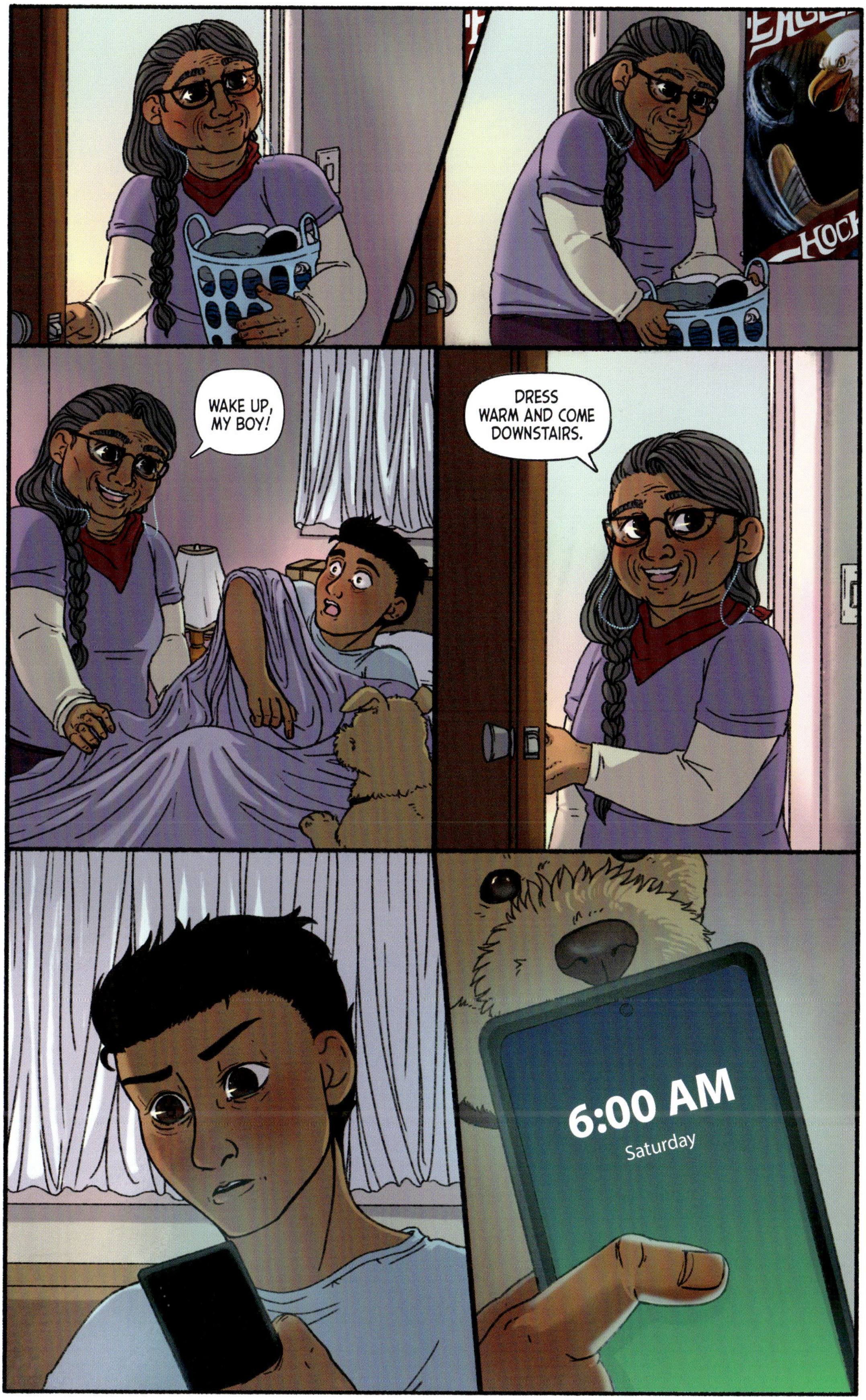
EAGLE
HOCK
WAKE UP, MY BOY!
DRESS WARM AND COME DOWNSTAIRS.
6:00 AM
Saturday

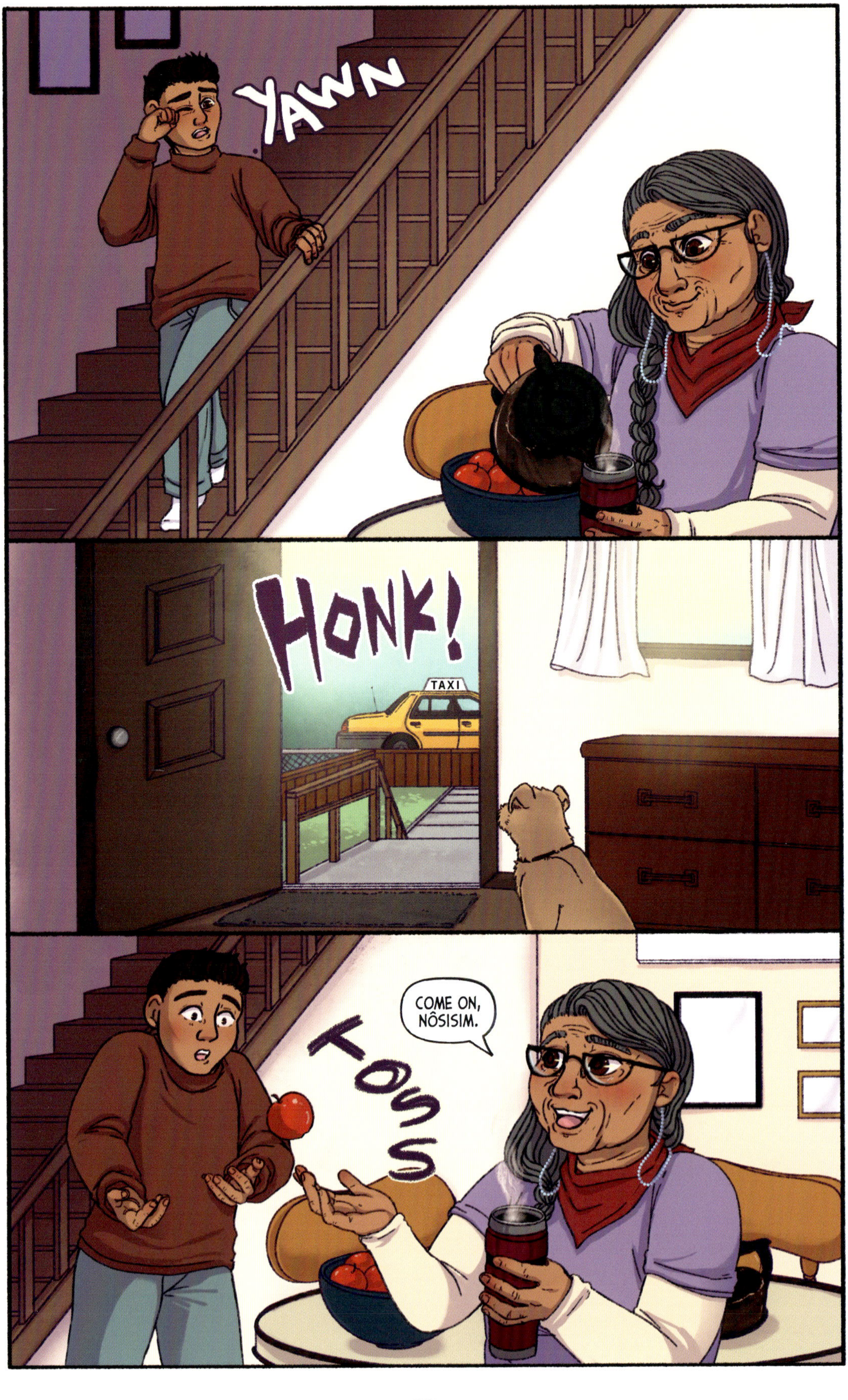
YAWN
HONK!
TAXI
COME ON, NÔSISIM.
TOSS

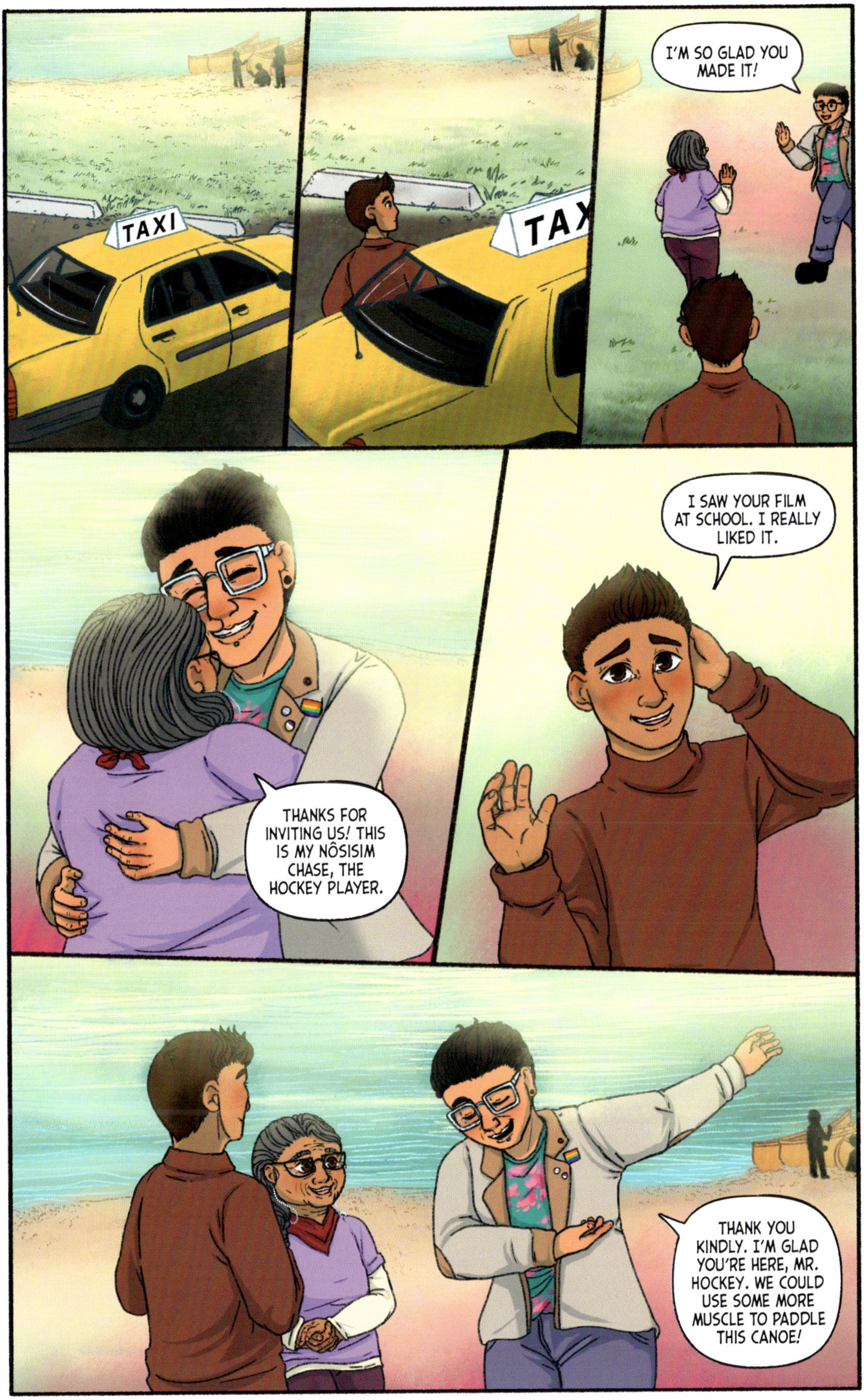
TAXI
TAX
I'M SO GLAD YOU MADE IT!
THANKS FOR INVITING US! THIS IS MY NÔSISIM CHASE, THE HOCKEY PLAYER.
I SAW YOUR FILM AT SCHOOL. I REALLY LIKED IT.
THANK YOU KINDLY. I'M GLAD YOU'RE HERE, MR. HOCKEY. WE COULD USE SOME MORE MUSCLE TO PADDLE THIS CANOE!

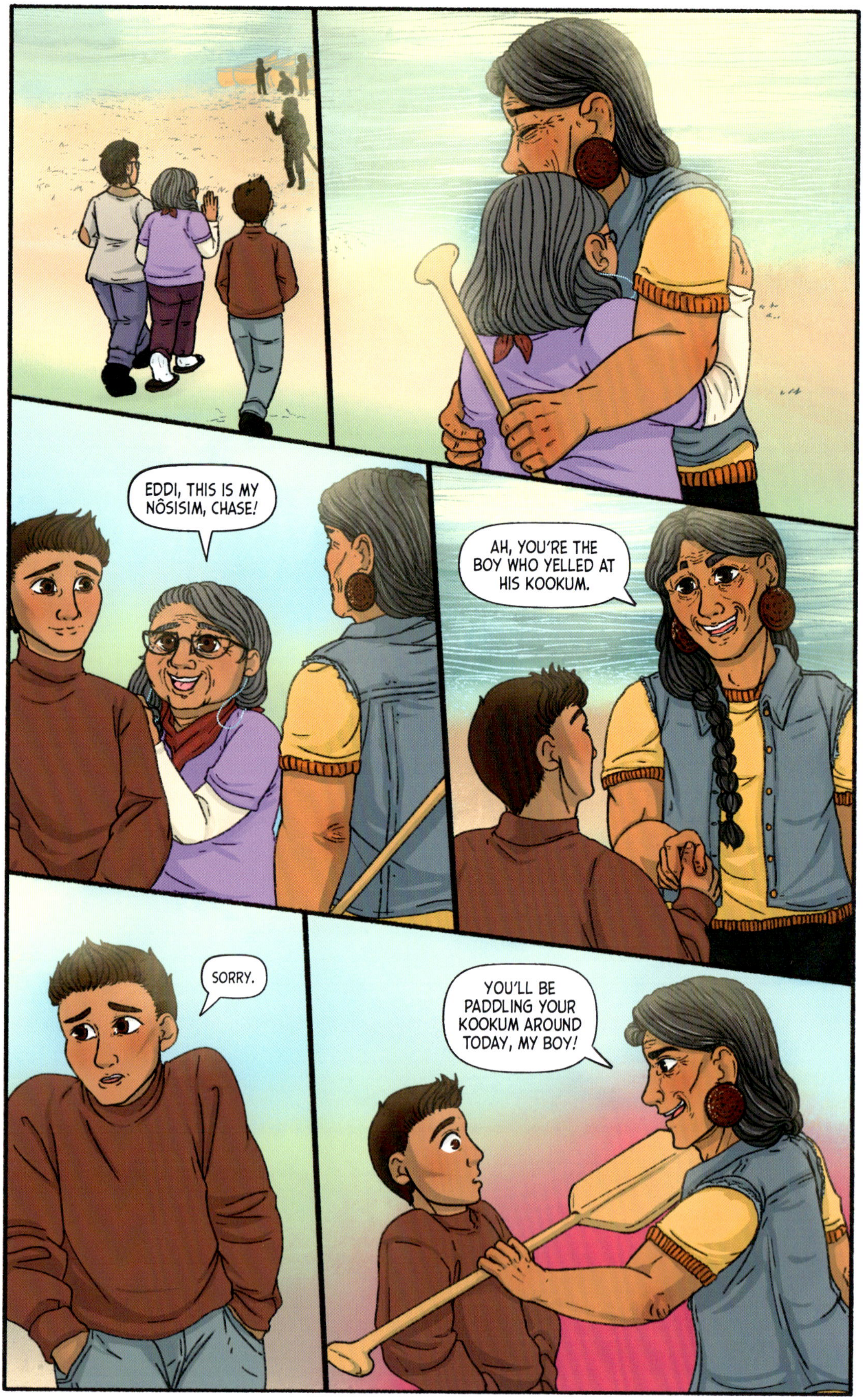
EDDI, THIS IS MY NÔSISIM, CHASE!
AH, YOU'RE THE BOY WHO YELLED AT HIS KOOKUM.
SORRY.
YOU'LL BE PADDLING YOUR KOOKUM AROUND TODAY, MY BOY!

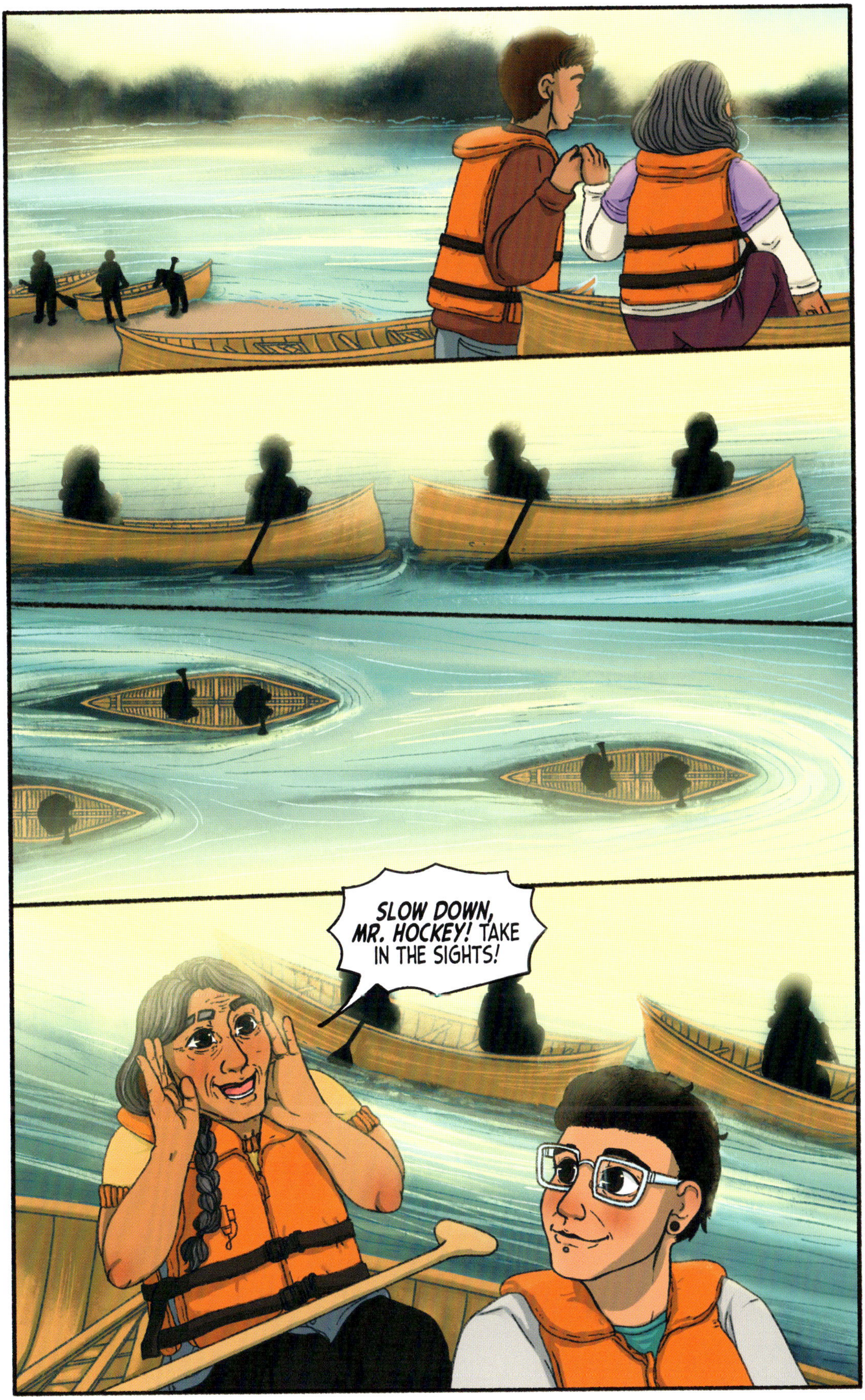
SLOW DOWN, MR. HOCKEY! TAKE IN THE SIGHTS!

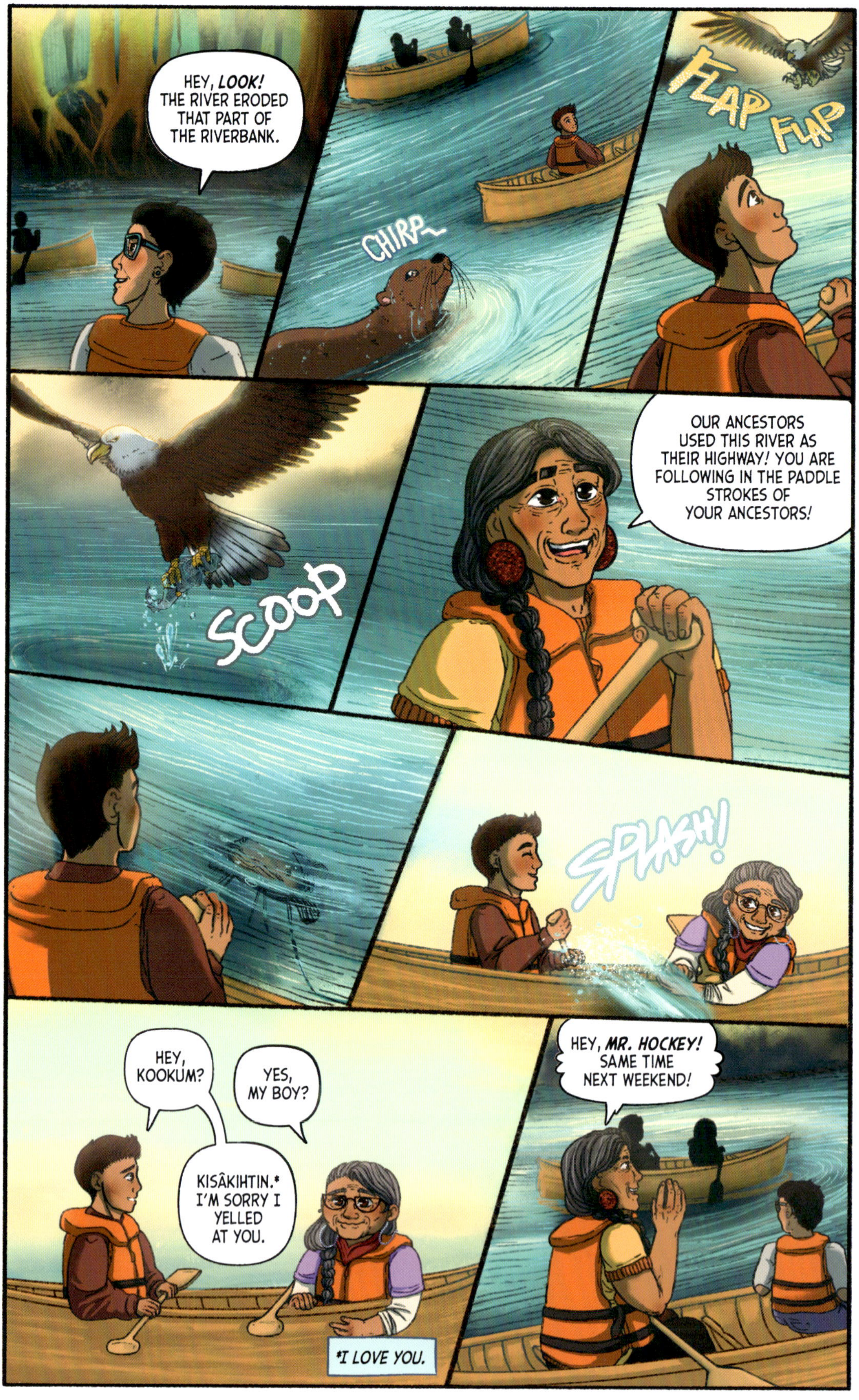
HEY, *LOOK!* THE RIVER ERODED THAT PART OF THE RIVERBANK.
CHIRP~
FLAP FLAP
SCOOP
OUR ANCESTORS USED THIS RIVER AS THEIR HIGHWAY! YOU ARE FOLLOWING IN THE PADDLE STROKES OF YOUR ANCESTORS!
SPLASH!
HEY, KOOKUM?
YES, MY BOY?
KISÂKIHTIN.* I'M SORRY I YELLED AT YOU.
*I LOVE YOU.
HEY, *MR. HOCKEY!* SAME TIME NEXT WEEKEND!

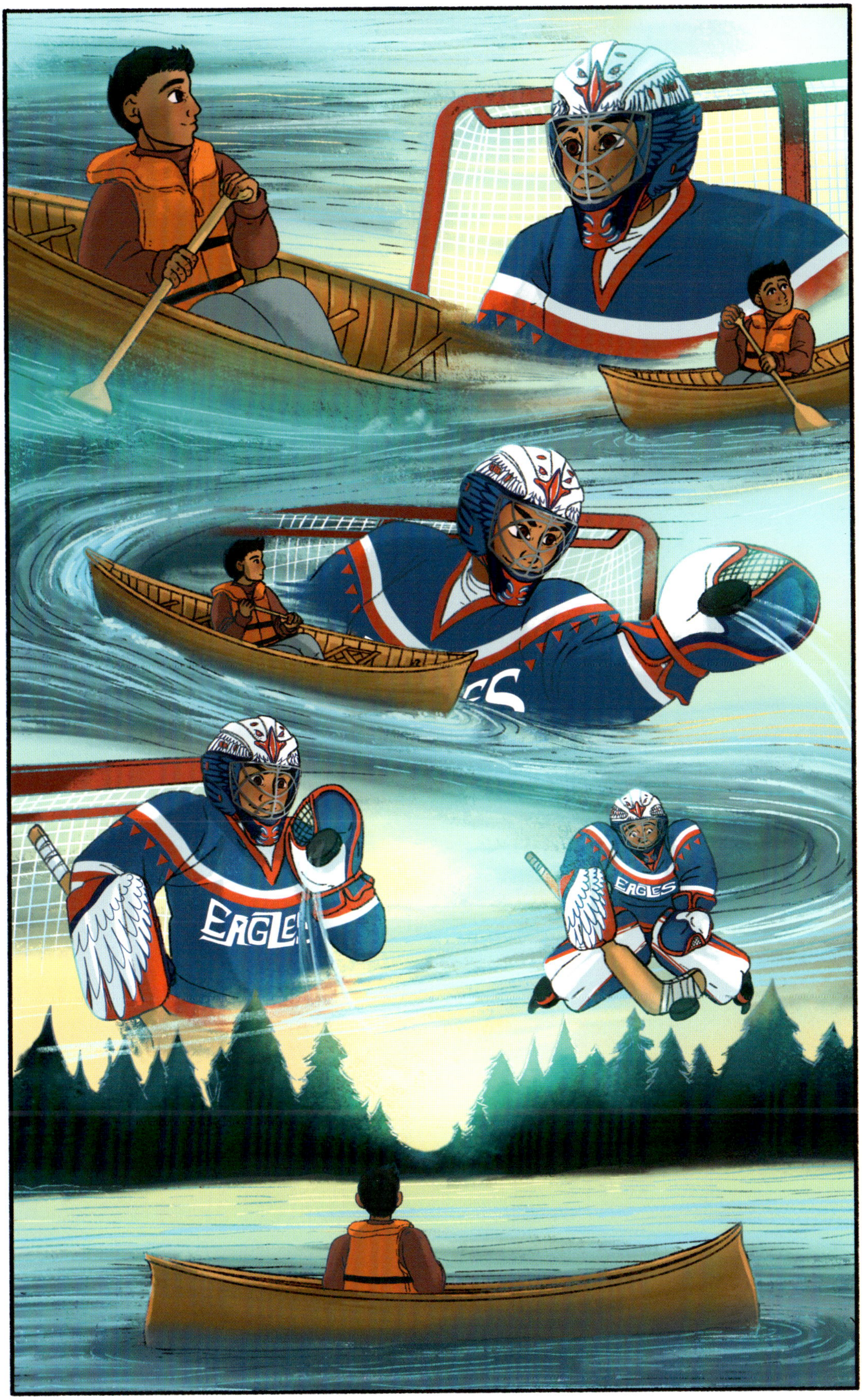
EAGLES

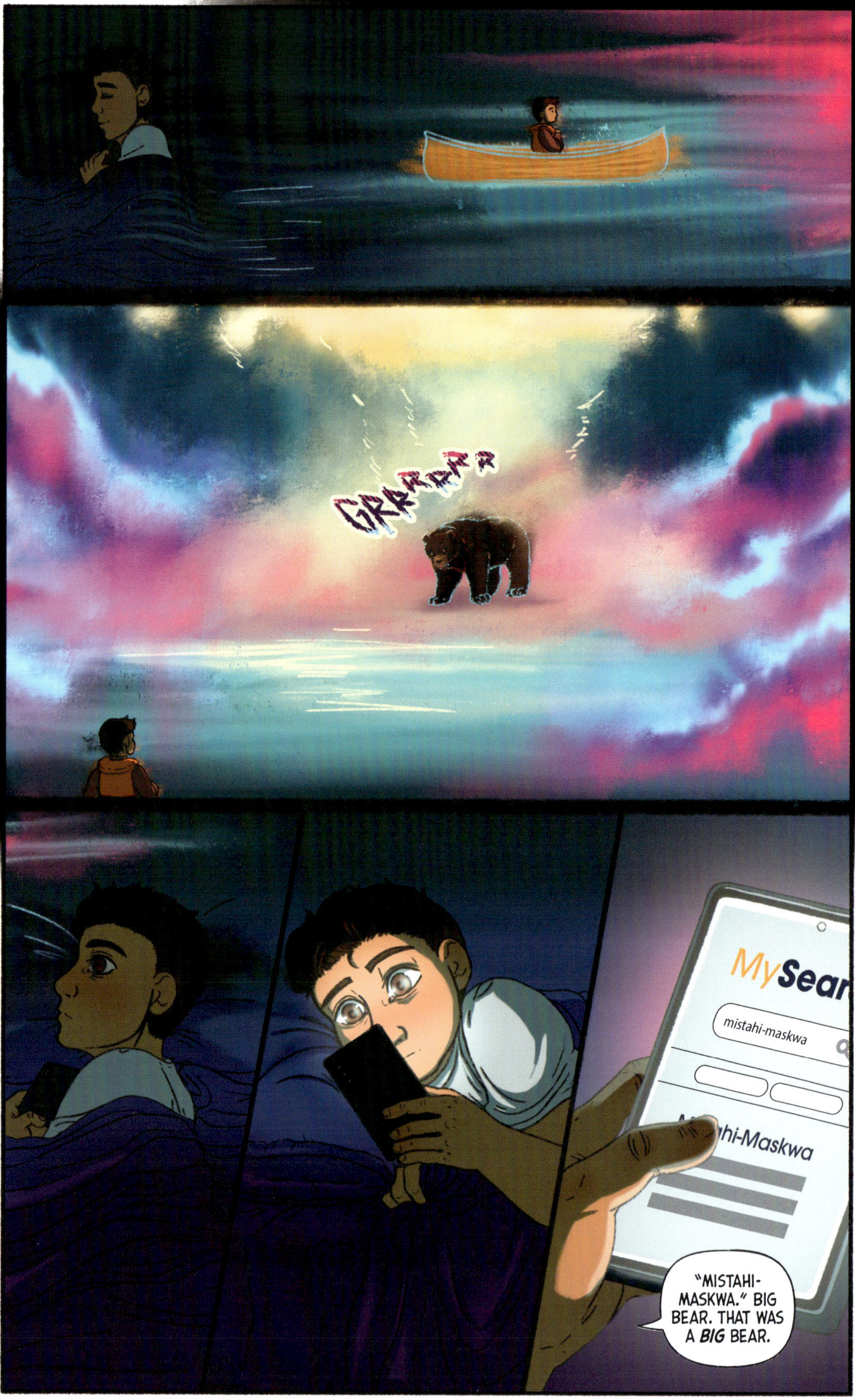
GRRRRR
MySear
mistahi-maskwa
hi-Maskwa
"MISTAHI-MASKWA." BIG BEAR. THAT WAS A *BIG* BEAR.

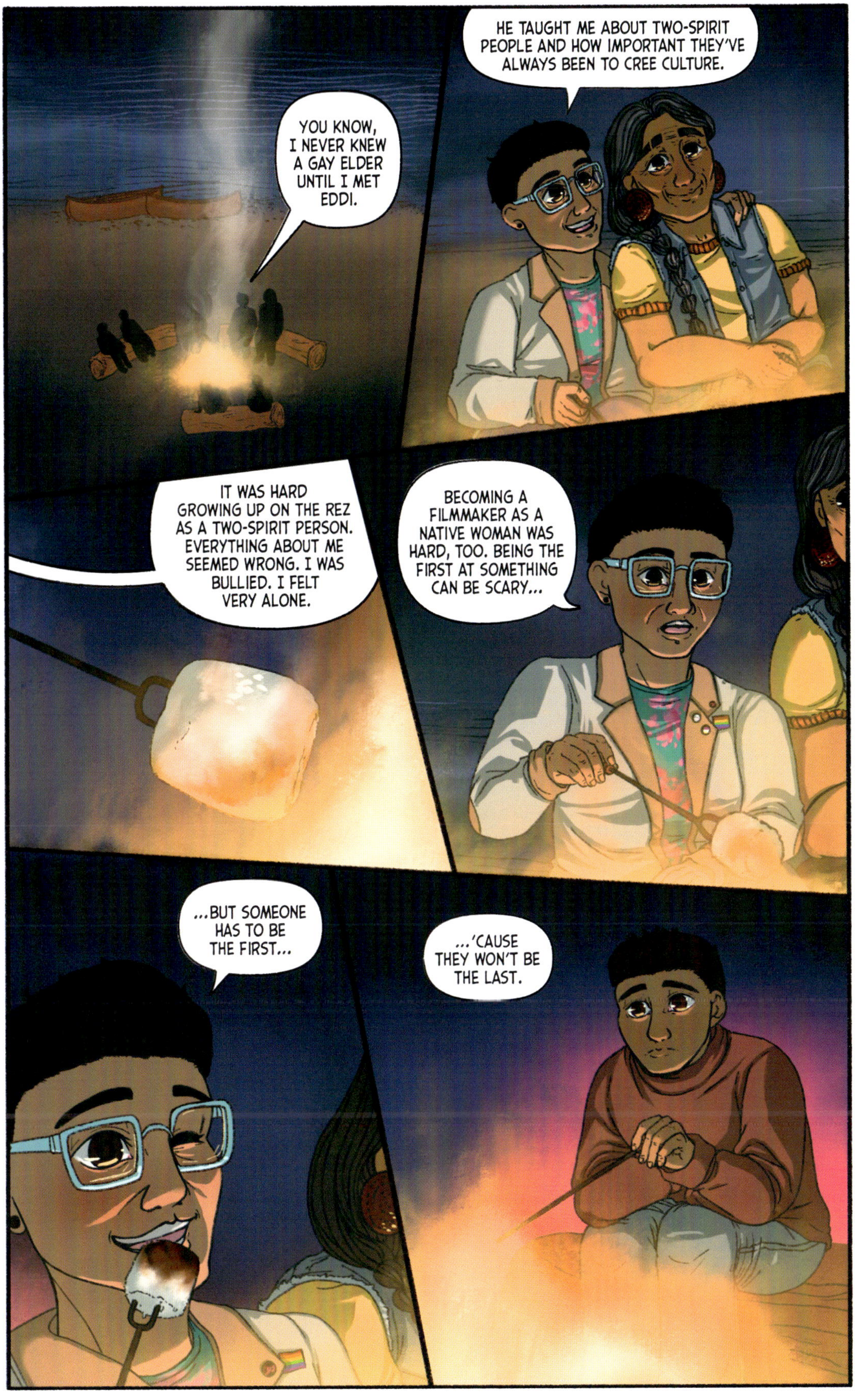
YOU KNOW, I NEVER KNEW A GAY ELDER UNTIL I MET EDDI.
HE TAUGHT ME ABOUT TWO-SPIRIT PEOPLE AND HOW IMPORTANT THEY'VE ALWAYS BEEN TO CREE CULTURE.
IT WAS HARD GROWING UP ON THE REZ AS A TWO-SPIRIT PERSON. EVERYTHING ABOUT ME SEEMED WRONG. I WAS BULLIED. I FELT VERY ALONE.
BECOMING A FILMMAKER AS A NATIVE WOMAN WAS HARD, TOO. BEING THE FIRST AT SOMETHING CAN BE SCARY...
...BUT SOMEONE HAS TO BE THE FIRST...
...'CAUSE THEY WON'T BE THE LAST.

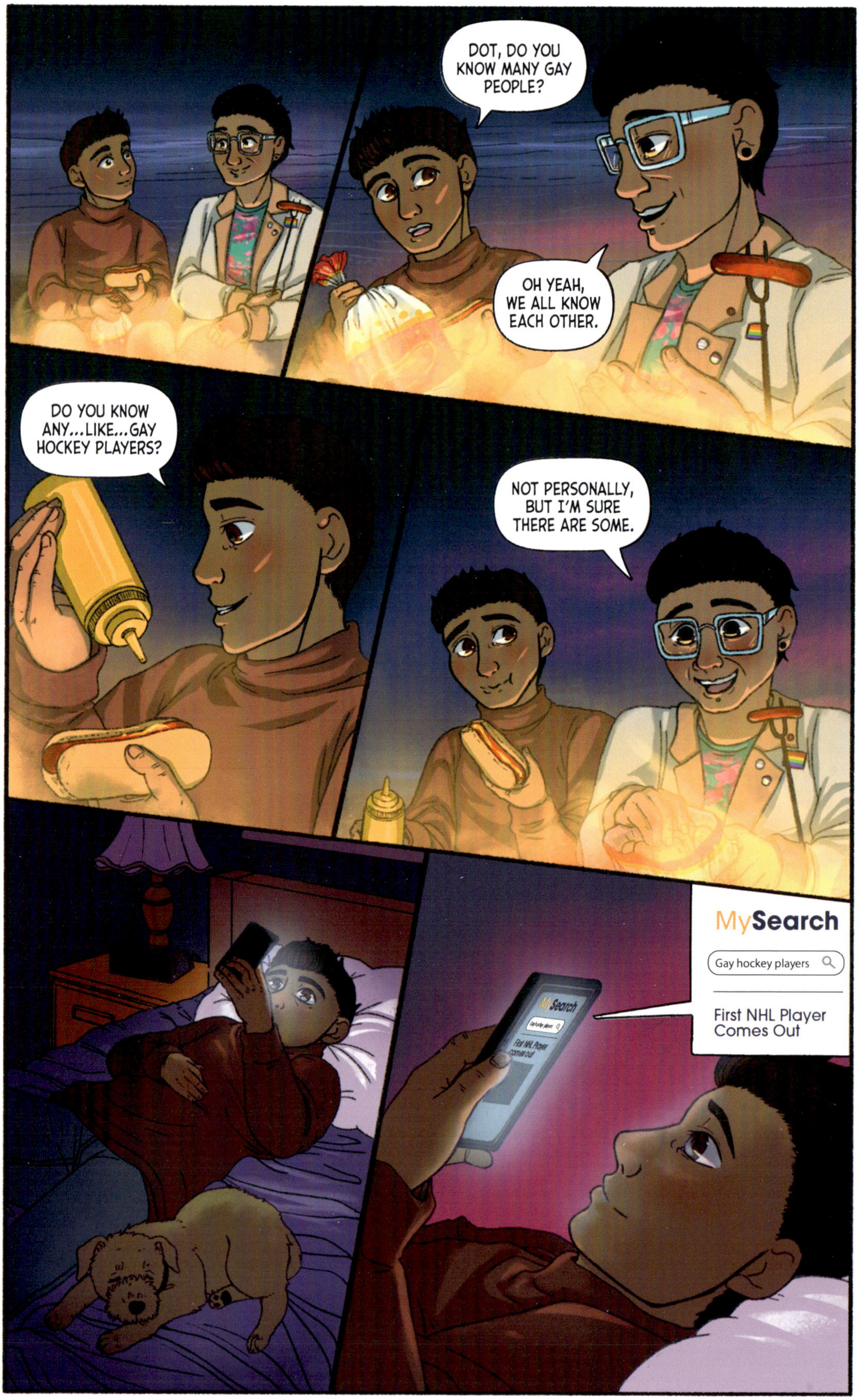
DOT, DO YOU KNOW MANY GAY PEOPLE?
OH YEAH, WE ALL KNOW EACH OTHER.
DO YOU KNOW ANY...LIKE...GAY HOCKEY PLAYERS?
NOT PERSONALLY, BUT I'M SURE THERE ARE SOME.
MySearch
Gay hockey players
First NHL Player Comes Out

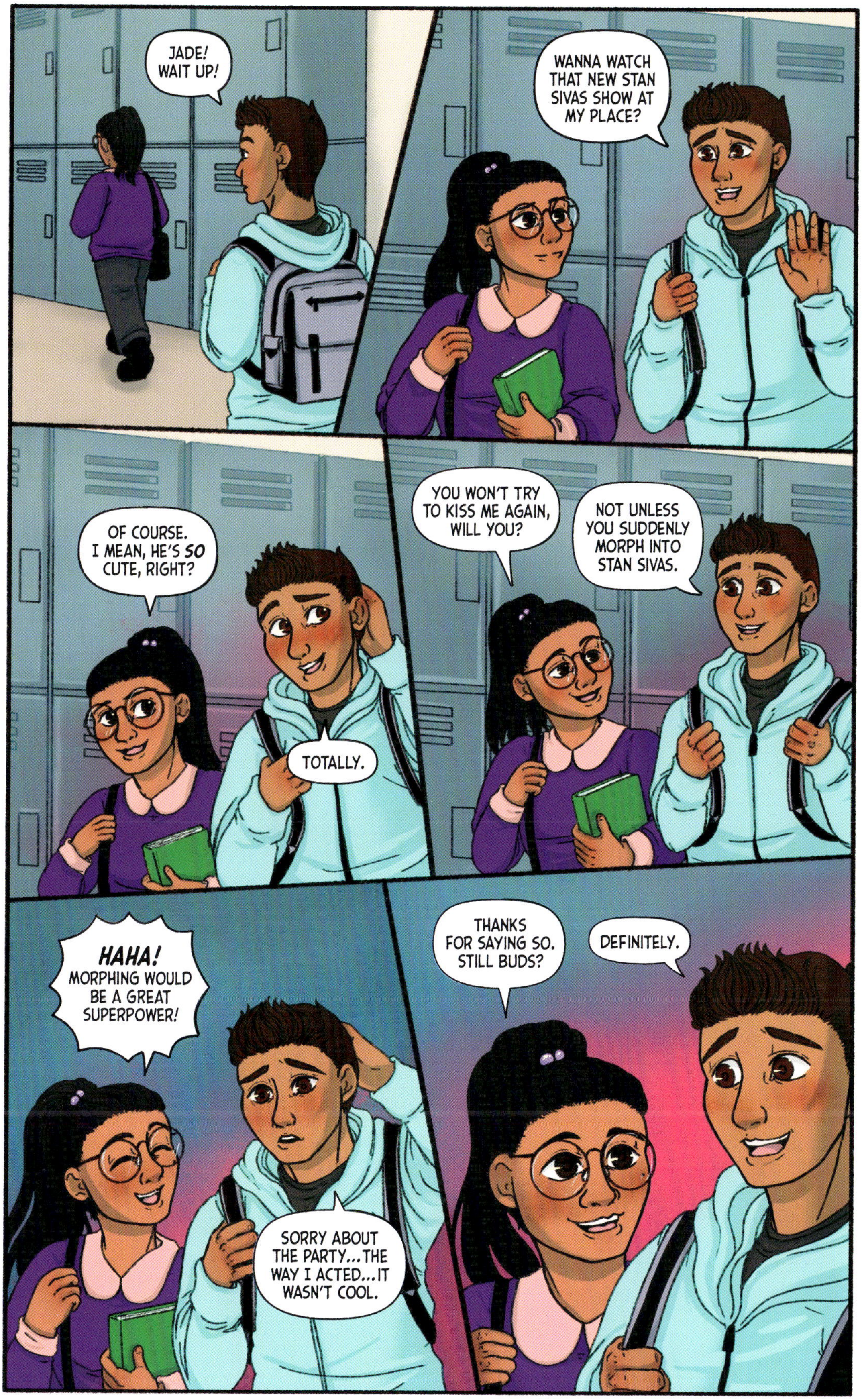
JADE! WAIT UP!
WANNA WATCH THAT NEW STAN SIVAS SHOW AT MY PLACE?
OF COURSE. I MEAN, HE'S SO CUTE, RIGHT?
TOTALLY.
YOU WON'T TRY TO KISS ME AGAIN, WILL YOU?
NOT UNLESS YOU SUDDENLY MORPH INTO STAN SIVAS.
HAHA! MORPHING WOULD BE A GREAT SUPERPOWER!
SORRY ABOUT THE PARTY...THE WAY I ACTED...IT WASN'T COOL.
THANKS FOR SAYING SO. STILL BUDS?
DEFINITELY.

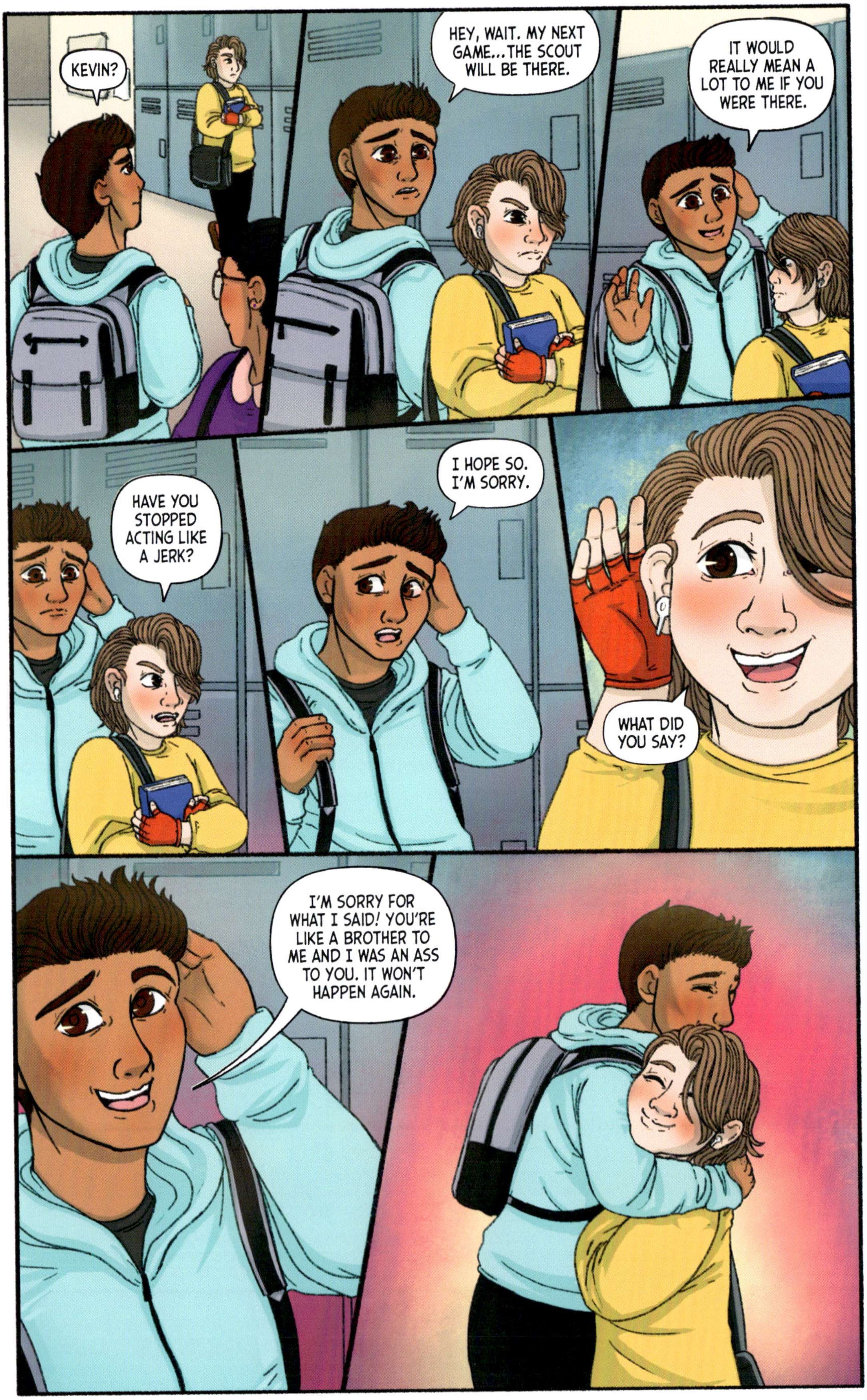
KEVIN?
HEY, WAIT. MY NEXT GAME...THE SCOUT WILL BE THERE.
IT WOULD REALLY MEAN A LOT TO ME IF YOU WERE THERE.
HAVE YOU STOPPED ACTING LIKE A JERK?
I HOPE SO. I'M SORRY.
WHAT DID YOU SAY?
I'M SORRY FOR WHAT I SAID! YOU'RE LIKE A BROTHER TO ME AND I WAS AN ASS TO YOU. IT WON'T HAPPEN AGAIN.

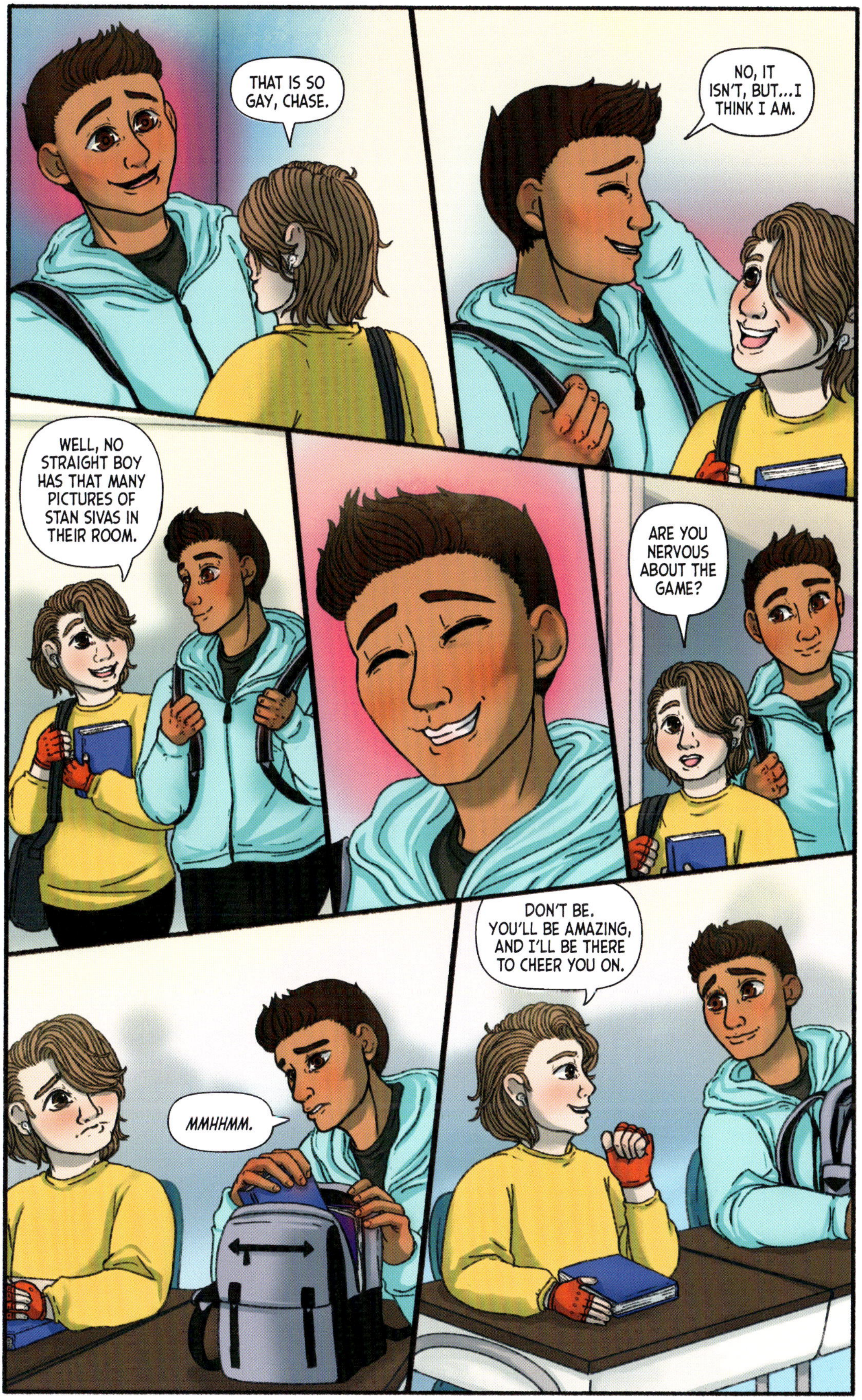
THAT IS SO GAY, CHASE.
NO, IT ISN'T, BUT...I THINK I AM.
WELL, NO STRAIGHT BOY HAS THAT MANY PICTURES OF STAN SIVAS IN THEIR ROOM.
ARE YOU NERVOUS ABOUT THE GAME?
MMHHMM.
DON'T BE. YOU'LL BE AMAZING, AND I'LL BE THERE TO CHEER YOU ON.

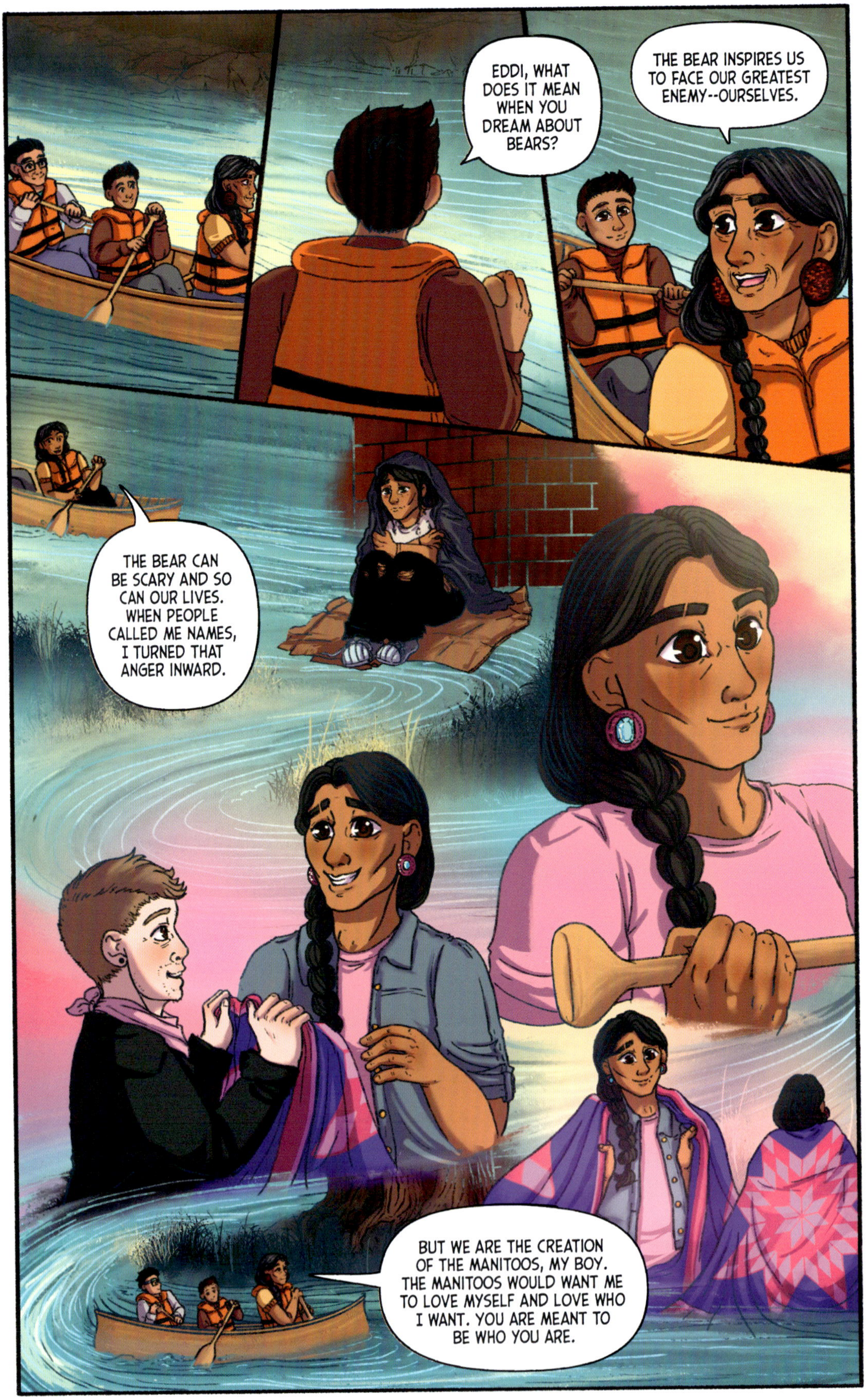
EDDI, WHAT DOES IT MEAN WHEN YOU DREAM ABOUT BEARS?
THE BEAR INSPIRES US TO FACE OUR GREATEST ENEMY--OURSELVES.
THE BEAR CAN BE SCARY AND SO CAN OUR LIVES. WHEN PEOPLE CALLED ME NAMES, I TURNED THAT ANGER INWARD.
BUT WE ARE THE CREATION OF THE MANITOOS, MY BOY. THE MANITOOS WOULD WANT ME TO LOVE MYSELF AND LOVE WHO I WANT. YOU ARE MEANT TO BE WHO YOU ARE.

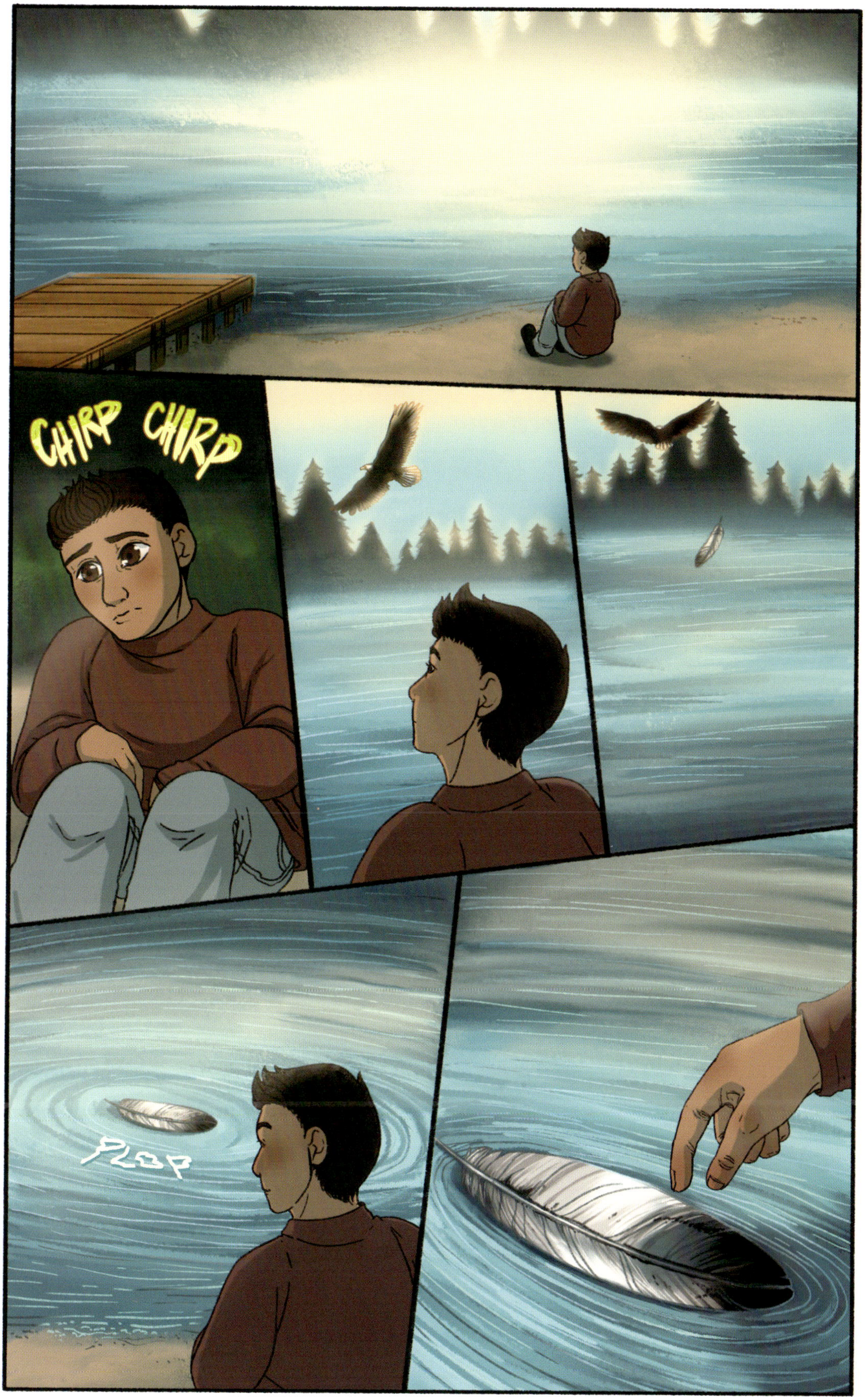
CHIRP CHIRP
PLOP

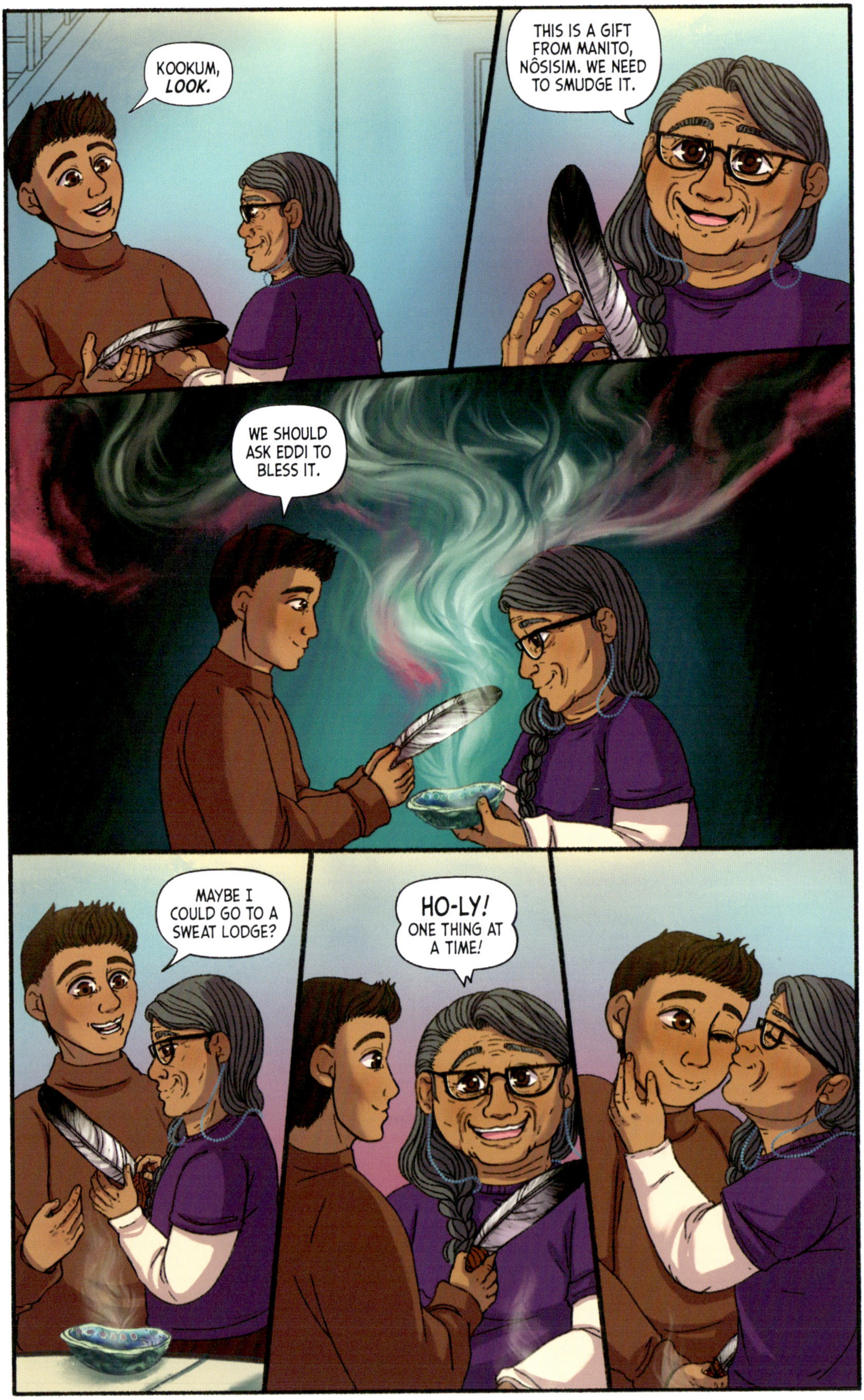
KOOKUM, *LOOK.*
THIS IS A GIFT FROM MANITO, NÔSISIM. WE NEED TO SMUDGE IT.
WE SHOULD ASK EDDI TO BLESS IT.
MAYBE I COULD GO TO A SWEAT LODGE?
HO-LY! ONE THING AT A TIME!

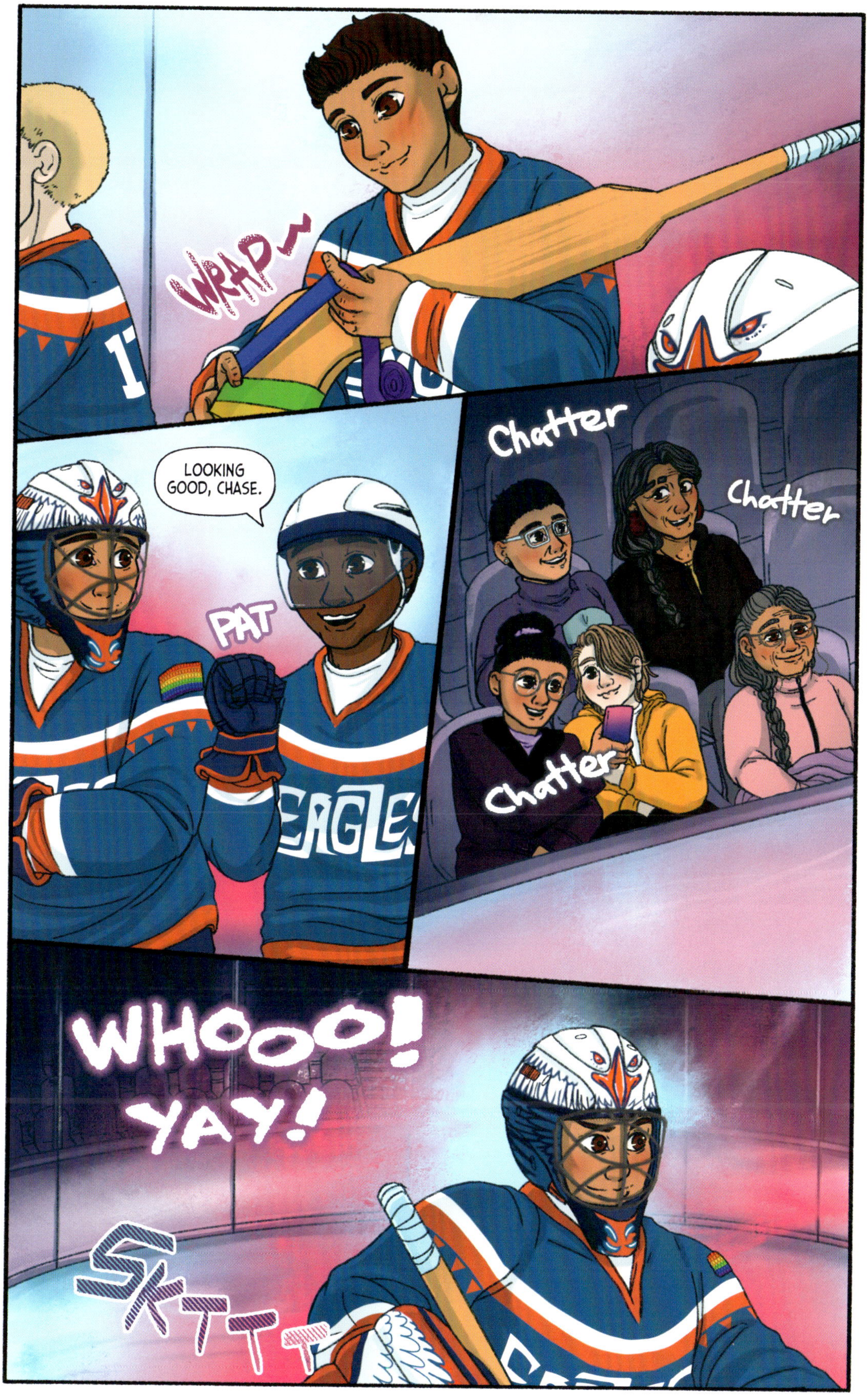
WRAP~
LOOKING GOOD, CHASE.
PAT
Chatter
Chatter
Chatter
WHOOO!
YAY!
SKTTTT

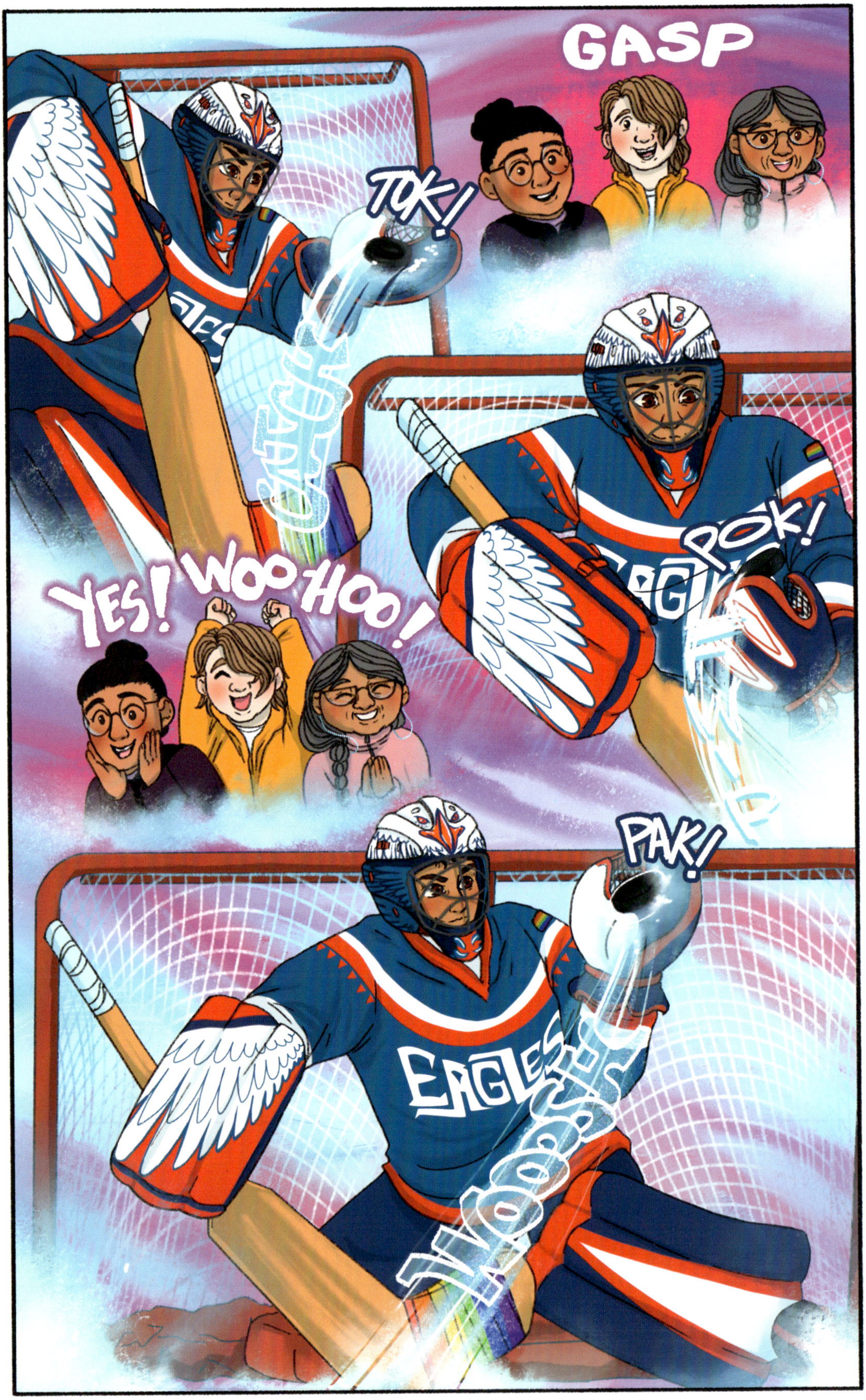
GASP
TOK!
YES! WOOHOO!
POK!
PAK!
EAGLES
WOOOSH

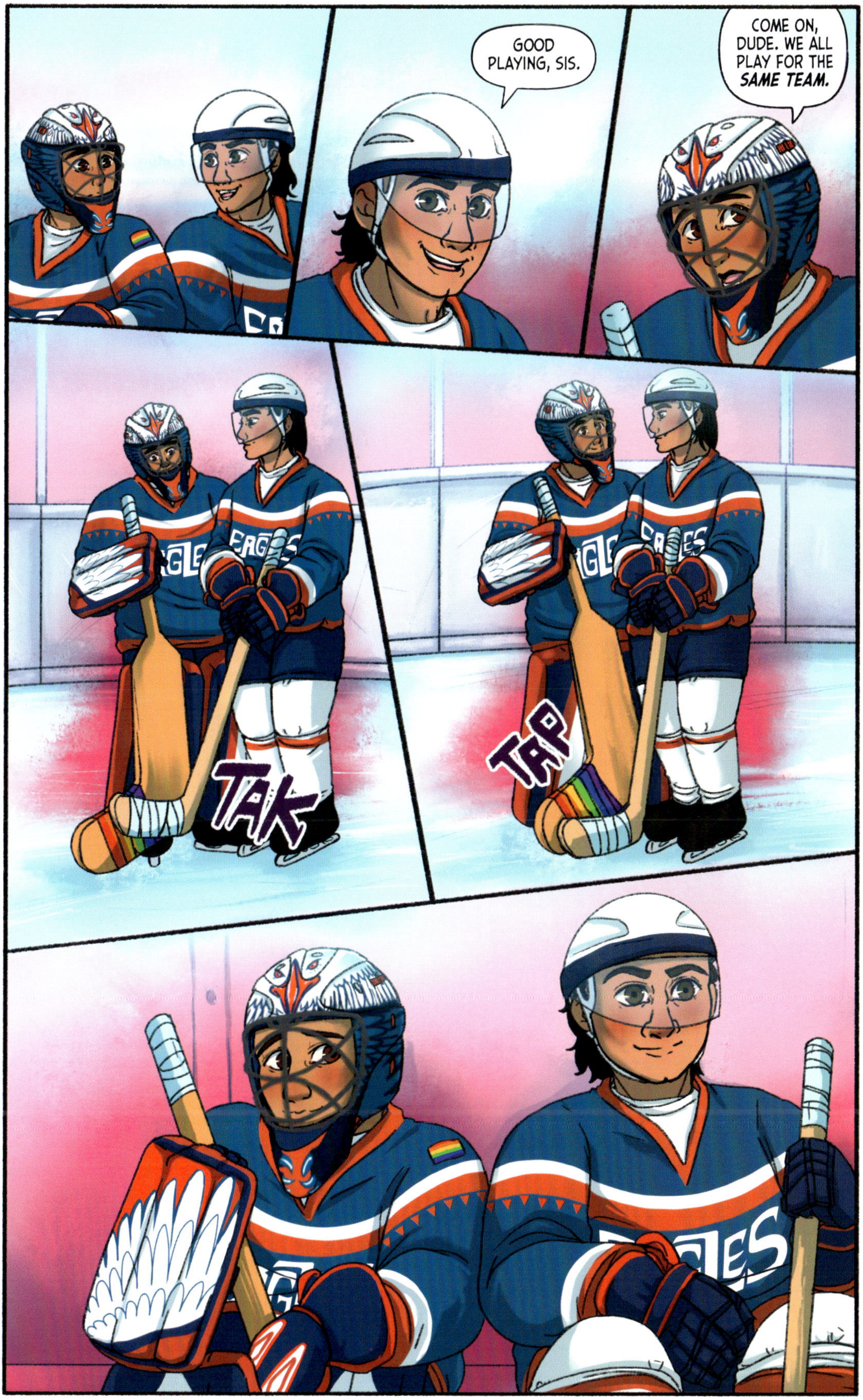
GOOD PLAYING, SIS.
COME ON, DUDE. WE ALL PLAY FOR THE ***SAME TEAM.***
TAK
TAP

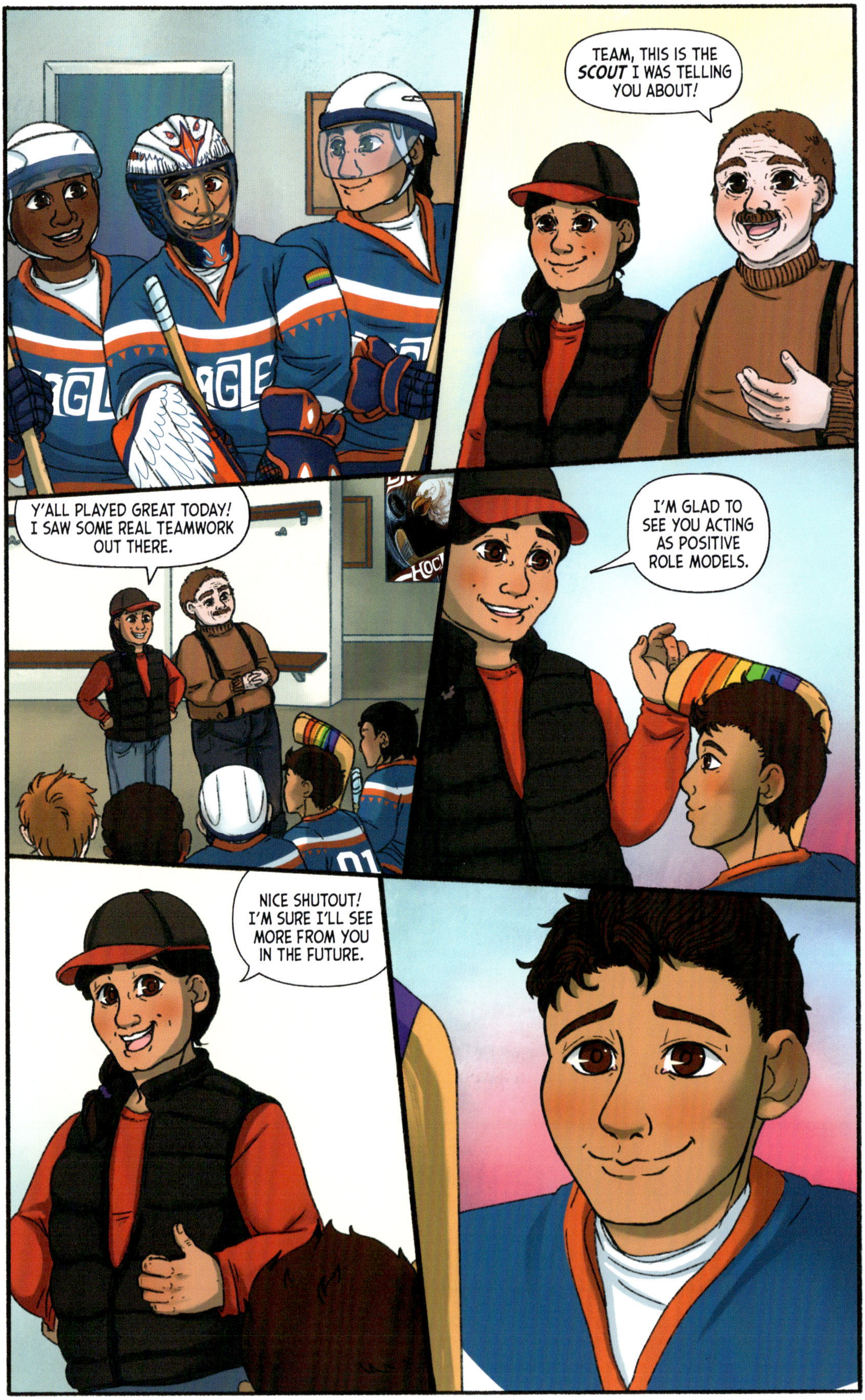
TEAM, THIS IS THE *SCOUT* I WAS TELLING YOU ABOUT!
Y'ALL PLAYED GREAT TODAY! I SAW SOME REAL TEAMWORK OUT THERE.
I'M GLAD TO SEE YOU ACTING AS POSITIVE ROLE MODELS.
NICE SHUTOUT! I'M SURE I'LL SEE MORE FROM YOU IN THE FUTURE.

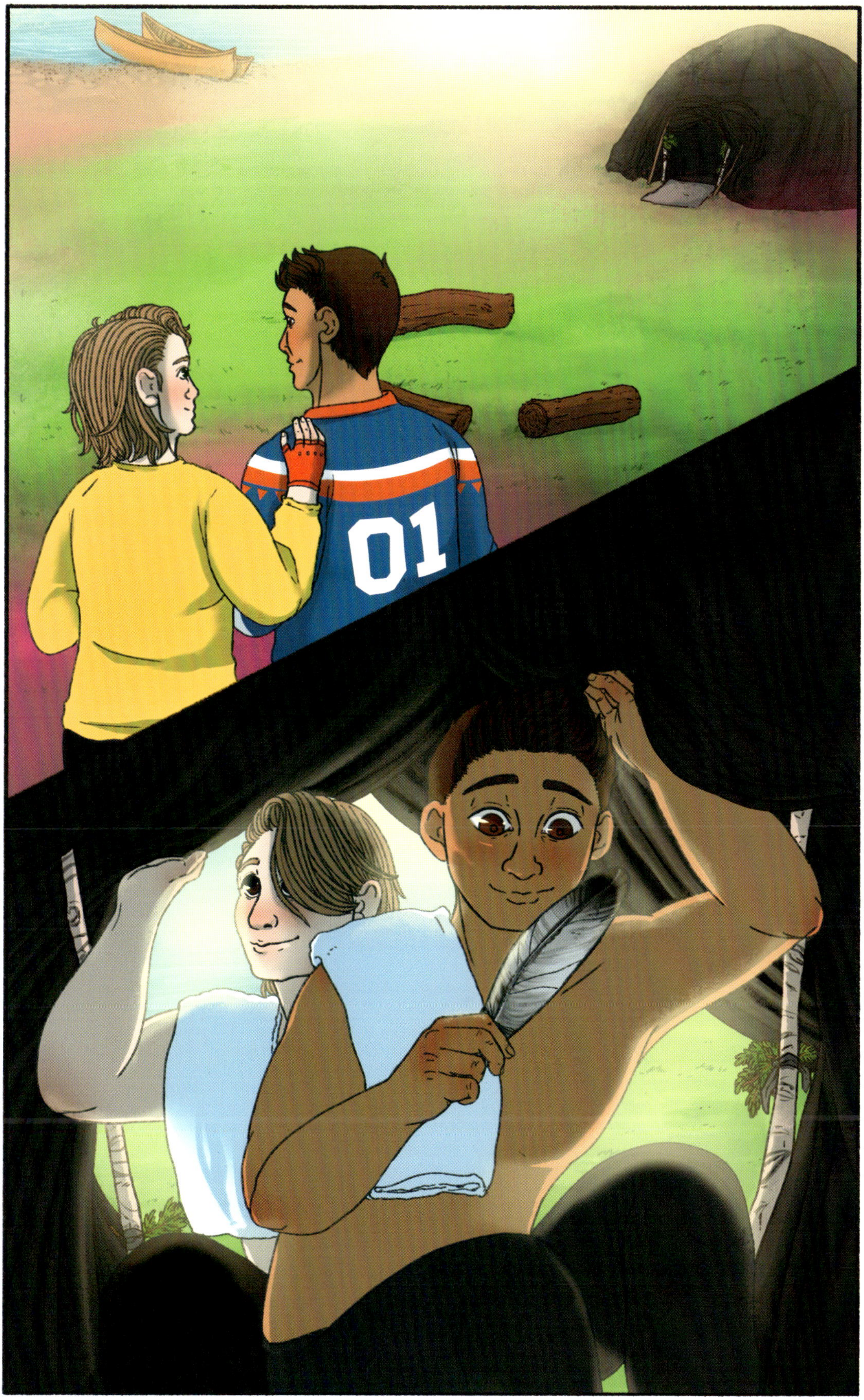
01

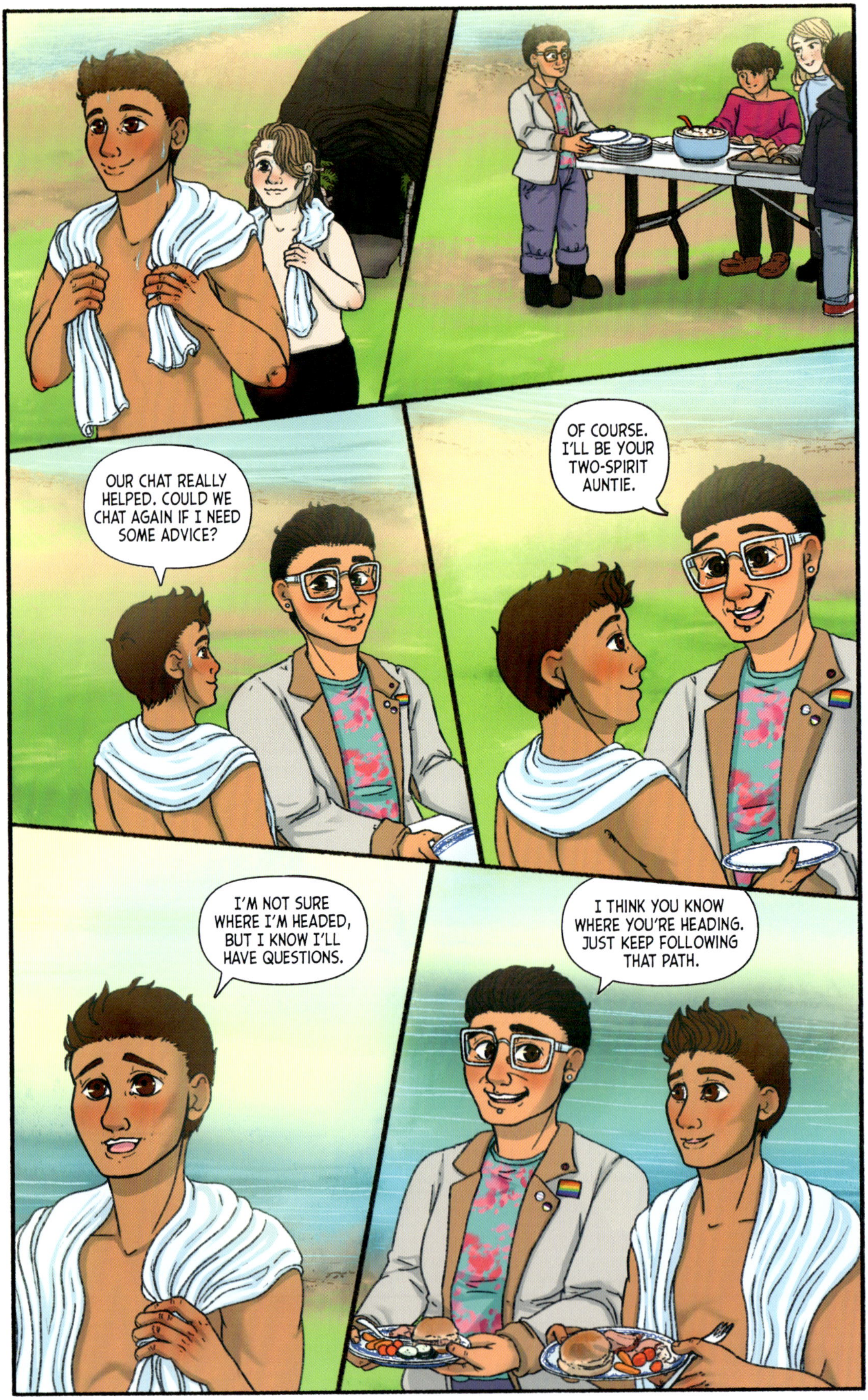
OUR CHAT REALLY HELPED. COULD WE CHAT AGAIN IF I NEED SOME ADVICE?
OF COURSE. I'LL BE YOUR TWO-SPIRIT AUNTIE.
I'M NOT SURE WHERE I'M HEADED, BUT I KNOW I'LL HAVE QUESTIONS.
I THINK YOU KNOW WHERE YOU'RE HEADING. JUST KEEP FOLLOWING THAT PATH.

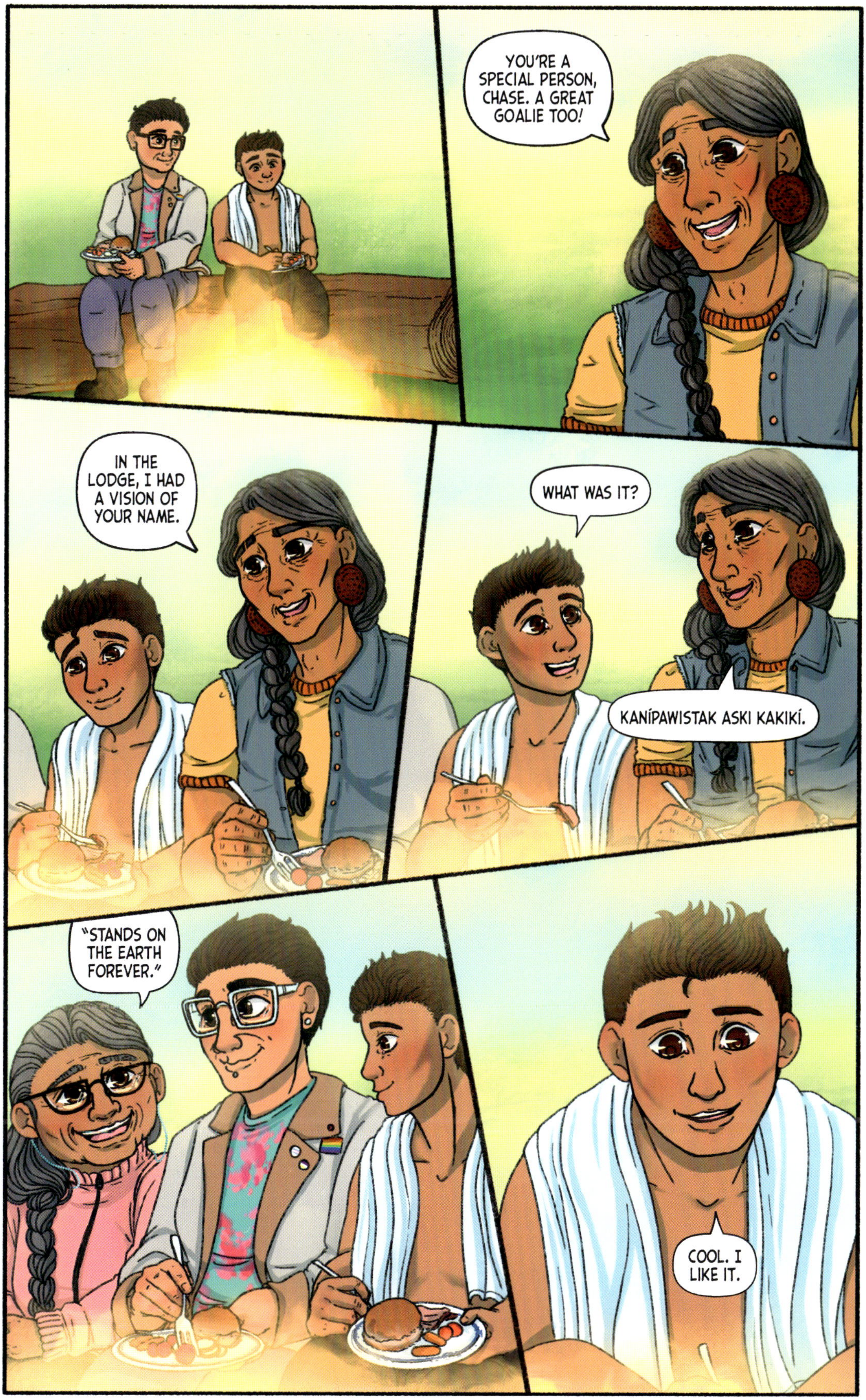
YOU'RE A SPECIAL PERSON, CHASE. A GREAT GOALIE TOO!
IN THE LODGE, I HAD A VISION OF YOUR NAME.
WHAT WAS IT?
KANÍPAWISTAK ASKI KAKIKÍ.
"STANDS ON THE EARTH FOREVER."
COOL. I LIKE IT.

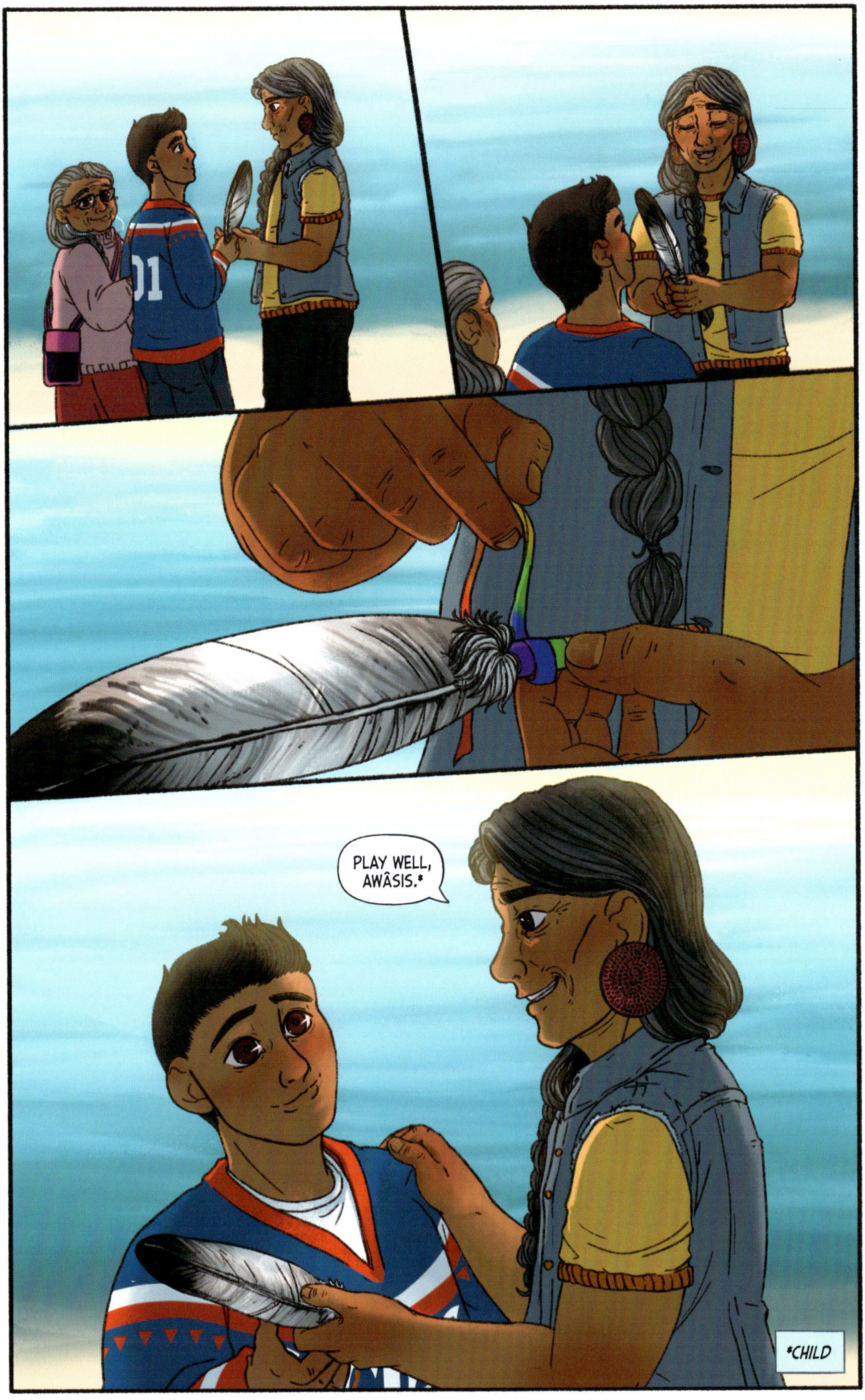
PLAY WELL,
AWÂSIS.*
*CHILD

A Word From the Authors

Chase's journey toward self-understanding and self-acceptance as an 2SLGBTQI+ youth is a common one. This is especially true for First Nations, Inuit, and Métis youth whose families and communities have been impacted by colonization. Although he experiences homophobia and toxic masculinity associated with sports culture, Chase is supported by family, friends, and his cultural identity. This allows Chase to use his gifts to create meaningful change within his community. Indigenous cultures around the world have a long history of inclusion within their families and communities. In 2015, late Ojibwe language specialist Roger Roulette said, "Ojibwe people believe that all children born have a role, a purpose, a destiny, and possess a divine gift. He/she (animate being) is who he/she (animate being) is supposed to be."

There are many ways we can support 2SLGBTQI+ youth in our communities:
- Adapt to the reality of your 2Spirit child
- Continue loving and nurturing your 2Spirit child
- Support 2Spirit gatherings
- Support chosen/surrogate 2Spirit families
- Create and support 2Spirit rites of passage
- Affirm personal gender identity, expression, and pronouns
- Include 2Spirit people in cultural, spiritual, political, and sporting events
- Provide 2Spirit-specific sexual health information

More information about 2Spirit/Indigenous LGBTQQIA+ people can be found at the 2 Spirits in Motion Society (2spiritsinmotion.com), 2Spirit Consultants (2spiritconsultants.ca), and 2-Spirited People of the 1st Nations (2spirits.org).

—Albert McLeod

I first heard Elder Albert McLeod speak at an annual event on suicide awareness. He described how Two-Spirit people are at risk for suicide due to homophobia, violence, cultural loss, isolation, and rejection. Together, we developed an action research project to produce a graphic novel based on the lived experiences of Two-Spirit people.

Two-Spirit Elders, parents, and youth shared their experiences of growing up and living in the world as Two-Spirit people. Each noted that accepting yourself and learning to live safely in the world were difficult milestones. All participants told us the most important reason for writing the graphic novel is for youth to see there is hope, and to let them know that they will find helpers on their paths.

Resources and support for 2SLGBTQI+ people can be found at Klinic Community Health (klinic.mb.ca), Kids Help Phone (kidshelpphone.ca), Rainbow Resource Centre (rainbowresourcecentre.org), Trans Lifeline (translifeline.org), and Velma's House (www.kanikanichihk.ca/velmas-house/).

—Elaine Mordoch

This story is a work of fiction. The likeness of Vanessa Tait has been used as inspiration for the character of Dot Footprint with their consent.

HighWater Press gratefully acknowledges the financial support of the Government of Canada and Canada Council for the Arts as well as the Province of Manitoba through the Department of Sport, Culture, Heritage and Tourism and the Manitoba Book Publishing Tax Credit for our publishing activities.

Funded by the Government of Canada
Financé par le gouvernement du Canada | Canada

Canada Council Conseil de arts
for the Arts du Canada

HighWater Press is an imprint of Portage & Main Press.
Printed and bound in Canada by Friesens
Interior design by Jennifer Lum
Cover design by Frank Reimer
Cover art by Alice RL
Lettering by Kielamel Sibal

Special thanks to the College of Nursing, Rady Faculty of Health Sciences, University of Manitoba, and Winnipeg Suicide Prevention Network, Winnipeg Regional Health Authority, for their funding and support.

Special thanks to the following individuals who contributed valuable input to this project: Elder Peetanacoot Nenakawekapo, Standing Strong Eagle Woman Elder Charlotte Nolin, Elder Barbara Bruce, Allen Contois, Tara Everett, Cynthia Flett, Martini Monkman, Samantha Orvis-Campbell, and Jacqueline Pelland.

With thanks to the graphic arts student focus group from the Met Centre for Arts & Technology, Seven Oaks Met, and Maples Met School (Winnipeg, MB) for their thoughtful feedback on the cover of this book.

Elaine Mordoch has designated 40% of her share of the royalties from this book to Velma's House, a safe house named in honour of the late Elder Velma Orvis, who dedicated her time and compassion to her community.

Library and Archives Canada Cataloguing in Publication
Title: Between the pipes / story by Albert McLeod ; with Elaine Mordoch and Sonya Ballantyne ; art by Alice RL.
Names: McLeod, Albert, author. | Mordoch, Elaine, contributor. | Ballantyne, Sonya, contributor. | RL, Alice, artist.
Description: In English with some text in Cree. Identifiers: Canadiana (print) 2024033325X | Canadiana (ebook) 20240384938 | ISBN 9781774921043 (softcover) | ISBN 9781774921050 (EPUB) | ISBN 9781774921067 (PDF)
Subjects: LCGFT: Graphic novels. Classification: LCC PN6733.M395 B48 2024 | DDC j741.5/971—dc23

27 26 25 24   1 2 3 4 5

This book was printed in North America by Friesens, the first FSC-certified printing company in Canada. With plants powered by hydroelectric and wind farms, the company is 100% employee-owned and is committed to minimizing its ecological footprint. It is printed on FSC-certified paper using vegetable-based inks and alcohol-free blanket wash.

MIX
Paper | Supporting responsible forestry
FSC www.fsc.org FSC® C016245

HIGHWATER PRESS
www.highwaterpress.com
Winnipeg, Manitoba
Treaty 1 Territory and homeland of the Métis Nation